A thread of desire tickled low in Patricia's abdomen and traveled upward to envelop her brain, and she wanted to be closer to him than was physically possible. She melted against him; her arms went to caress his back, to feel the muscles move beneath his skin, to hold him nearer. Her breath became short, and she answered the probing of his kiss with a hunger she hadn't known she owned. She wanted nothing more than to have Derrick then and there, in the deepening dark of the evening, on the soft and pungent pine....

ABOUT THE AUTHOR

Kami Lane didn't always know that she wanted to be a writer, but had an early indication that she would be successful when she sold the very first story she ever wrote. Since that time she's been committed to her craft, and finds that writing is a fascinating, compulsive, and unending endeavor.

Fantasy Lover

KAMI LANE

Harlequin Books

TORONTO • NEW YORK • LONDON
AMSTERDAM • PARIS • SYDNEY • HAMBURG
STOCKHOLM • ATHENS • TOKYO • MILAN

For that fool who rushed in
and turned out
to be an angel anyway:
My husband, Rod

Published March 1984

ISBN 0-373-16047-X

Printed in Canada

Chapter One

"Turn your head a little more to the right, Patricia," Jerome said. "Give us a little more taxi."

Patricia turned her head slightly, widened her stance, and someone turned on the fan. Her freshly washed hair swirled in a russet cloud behind her, and tendrils, caught by the updraft rising from a strategically placed baffle, danced high. The chiffon scarf, looped around her throat, did an intricate choreography. Her head was in profile to the camera and she had no expression on her face: no smile, no frown. Her eyes were lifted to gaze into the distance as if she could see the ultimate answer to everything she would ever need.

Nothing could be farther from the truth. What she saw was the stained plaster wall of the studio, but she could feel the nearness of the personal and private man of her dreams, knew he was only a half-thought away and would be there the moment she wanted him.

"Give us you secret smile. Patricia," Jerome said.

She let him appear When he did, her lips obeyed the photographer and she suddenly looked as if she were on the verge of having her most passionate yearnings satisfied.

"Ah, *La Gioconda*," Jerome said. "The Mona Lisa. You do that better than anyone, Pat."

Her mouth almost broke from the small pleased tilt into a grin. If Jerome knew what went on in her mind, he'd think she was crazy. Nothing from real life gave her the ability to project an expression of loving and being loved, of desiring and being desired. That quality came from a fantasy world she'd built for herself.

She'd begun to create her dreamworld two years ago. She hadn't needed it earlier in her career because then she'd thought the real world was wonderful and beautiful and able to give her all she wanted. But she'd been relieved of those ideas. Bart had been married and had lied to her. He'd always lied to her. He'd used her.

After one of her discussions with him—or should it be called an argument?—he'd said she wasn't worth his time or effort, and he'd gone angrily, saying he'd never phone her again. She never should have become involved with Bartholomew VanStang. He was cynical, unprincipled, deceitful, and manipulative—as little like the man in her fantasy as anyone could be. But she hadn't known that when she met him.

Alone and rejected, she'd needed something to keep her going, something to replace her lost faith and trust in humanity; so she'd begun to dream. Now her fantasy was intricate and complete, and she could drift in and out of it as the situation required. She rarely missed any of the photographer's directions and was usually aware of things going on around her, but she could dip into her imaginary world instantly to get a proper expression. Lately, though, she often took too long to come out of it, and sometimes she dropped into it without any reason. She shouldn't allow that to happen, she knew.

Her face had lapsed into a solemn expression with her thoughts. "You've lost it. Patricia," Jerome said. "Lower your eyes, give us the smile."

She did and saw her fantasy lover coming toward her He didn't have a name—a name would destroy the illusion. "I love you," he whispered, but he stayed tantalizingly out of her reach, out of focus of the camera. "I never knew what love was until I met you." At those words her lips swelled and parted in anticipation of a kiss.

"That's it," Jerome said. "Fantastic." The camera clicked and the film whirred to advance. "Now joy, Patricia. Ecstasy. The fulfillment every woman wants."

Her eyes closed and her head tipped backward to make her mouth more accessible. Her blood pulsed more quickly.

"Rapture," Jerome said softly, not wanting to break her concentration.

Her eyes, cloudy with desire and need, opened. He came toward her. His every step was an enchantment, and every glance at her out of his intense eyes was an invitation to delights beyond her dreams. "Come to me," she wanted to say. The words trembled on the tip of her tongue.

"This way, Pat. Turn more this way."

She did, and he moved to stay within her line of vision. In a moment he would take the last step toward her, take her into his arms, and she would know the reason for living.

"Perfect," Jerome breathed.

His mouth touched hers, possessed her, and made her weak. Her arms lifted and spread the winglike sleeves of the gown, letting them catch the channeled air

"Okay, that wraps it up," Jerome said in a normal tone. "Thanks, Pat. Terrific."

"I can't live without you," her dream lover said. "Come with me." She reached to take his hand and started to move toward him.

"Patricia," Jerome said sharply. "We're done. It was a great session. You can change now."

Her eyes came into focus, he disappeared, and she came back to earth with mind-stunning abruptness. She felt the lack of mechanical wind, saw Jerome taking film out of his camera, and heard the scrape of a lighting tower being shoved out of the way. "Oh," she said. "Okay, Jerome."

The photographer grinned at her. "You're getting better each time we work together, Pat. I don't know how you do it."

If he knew, he'd probably rush her to the nearest psychiatrist. She'd thought about going to a doctor because her fantasy world was breaking into real life more often. She knew she should control her dreams. It was only when she worked that she needed them, but now she was dreaming without having to. She wished she hadn't begun, because she didn't know how to stop.

"I hope you get the Merchand contract," Jerome was saying. "It would be a long one, and you would be working for only one line. You'd become a top model. And you're perfect for them. Not only are you gorgeous, you're the most responsive model I've ever worked with."

"Thanks, Jerome." She smiled at him. "I hope I get it, too."

"When will you know?"

"I don't know. In a week or so, I think. I meet with

the board of directors this afternoon. After they interview all the finalists, they'll make their decision, and while they mull it over, I'm going away."

"Going on a vacation, huh?"

"Sort of."

"Lucky you," he said enviously as she went into the dressing room.

She took off the makeup she'd used for the sitting, redid it more subtly, then pulled her hair into a twist that exposed the classic bone structure of her face. After she put on an electric-blue suit that matched the blue of her eyes, she looked elegant, chic, and sophisticated—just right for Merchand. She hoped they thought so. She wanted to represent the company for its maiden venture into the cosmetic field. The salary would be extravagant, and she needed the money.

Two other models were under consideration for the position: a young honey-blonde and a sensuous-looking brunette. Whether they'd already been seen by the board or had it yet to go through, she didn't know; she just knew she had to, and within minutes. She was nervous at the thought of meeting so many powerful businessmen at one time and having to please them. And the things she'd heard about Derrick Merchand led her to believe he wouldn't be easy. She'd never met him, but she'd read snips in columns and heard others talk about him. He was a handsome sought-after bachelor, a decisive, demanding executive leader, and was tremendously difficult to please.

When she reached the Merchand Corporation office building, she was told she had to wait. As she idly leafed through a magazine and tried to keep her nerves under control, she told herself she didn't have to land the contract. But last year her mother's hospital bills had piled up. She had to have two operations and around-the-clock care, and she was still in therapy. Yet, Martha was doing fine. The doctors were pretty sure they'd got all the cancer, and that was what was important. But the medical bills, along with Pat's own debts, added up to a formidable mountain of owed money. If she didn't get the Merchand contract, she'd have to sell Rose's cottage on Otter Key. Her aunt Rose had bequeathed it to her, telling Pat's father it would be silly for the property to go through probate twice, and she knew he'd leave it to his only offspring. Parnell had hated to ask his daughter for help. He was a proud man. He'd liquidated most of his assets, and still he'd had to ask Patricia to contribute. If she couldn't help, they'd lose their home.

"Miss Dayton," the receptionist said. "You may go in now."

Pat jumped as if she'd heard a gunshot. "Am I—? Is—? Have the—?" She wanted some information, but she was making a pitiful attempt to get it.

"You're the last," the woman said. "One came this morning, one just after noon, and now you."

She made her mouth form an O, then tried again. "Did they—? Was—?"

"No decision has been made yet, but if you want to be considered, I suggest you don't keep them waiting. Mr Merchand is planning to leave on a trip this evening and he won't look kindly on anyone delaying his schedule."

"Where?" she asked. Though it was only one word, she managed to get an entire question out.

"This way." She led Patricia toward a door. "Don't worry too much about the audition." she said.

"Mr. Merchand?   " Pat asked apprehensively.

"He isn't an ogre. He won't bite you." She smiled. "He'll just growl a little."

Pat returned the smile. "Thanks." But her tension didn't lessen an iota, and she was tempted to escape into fantasy.

When she went into the boardroom, every head turned toward her. The board members were seated on either side of a long polished mahogany table. Some of them smiled, some frowned—and each inspected her. The man at the head of the table must be Derrick Merchand, she thought as she let her gaze flick past him. Her glance was brief and told her only that he was younger than she supposed he would be. She wanted to study him, as he was the chairman of the board, the president of Merchand Corporation, and he held the power of the final word about who would represent his company. But she didn't let her gaze dwell on him. She didn't want to appear too eager or as if she were pleading.

"Would you take the platform, please," he said. It was more an order than a request. "Behind you," he said.

A temporary stage had been built along one end of the room. It was equipped with a number of props, a closed circuit television camera, and a microphone. She went to it, and as she did a cameraman moved from a corner of the room to join her.

"Say something," Merchand said.

"I beg your pardon?" She turned toward him, but lights that had been set up to flood the makeshift platform came on, and she couldn't see anything past the glare in her eyes.

"Say something," he repeated. "If your voice is impossible, so are you. We don't want to go to the expense of getting someone to represent us, then have to do voice-overs to disguise a dreadful sound. Say something."

"When in the course of human events...", she began.

"Something else," he said. "Something with emotion and feeling. Even if you only talk about yourself and your career. I haven't met a model yet who didn't enjoy that and get wonderfully emotional about it."

He had a surly disposition, Patricia decided, and not a good opinion of people in her profession.

"We're waiting, Miss Dayton."

She looked into the curtain of light. "'O serpent heart,'" she began. The Shakespearian quotation, reviling exterior beauty that hides an underlying ugliness of spirit, seemed particularly appropriate to her. Merchand wasn't the least bit compassionate, and though she still couldn't see him to know if his looks fit the description, she directed her incensed recitation straight at him. As she finished her chin tilted regally into the air.

There was silence for a few seconds, then Merchand's voice broke into it. "Well. An aspiring actress, I believe."

"No, not at all. But you said say something with emotion, and that speech came to mind. I was in *Romeo and Juliet.*"

"Juliet, no doubt," he said dryly.

"Actually, no. I was the nurse." She tried to see through the mask of light and couldn't, so she gave a haughty stare to where she thought Merchand was seated.

A light chuckle came from one of the seats.

"At least your voice isn't impossible," Merchand said. "Let's see how you look."

For at least an hour she was moved around on the

platform, made to turn this way and that, smile, look solemn, sensuous, serious, happy, surprised. She was kept so busy, she didn't have a chance to drop into fantasy.

Only twice did Merchand speak. "Take down your hair," he said about halfway through the session. She did. And later he told her to take off her jacket.

She held a parasol, a bottle of Merchand perfume, Merchand cream, Merchand deodorant, and Merchand lip color, eye shadow, and mascara. She was beginning to wilt under the close, hot lights before the session was over. During the entire time she could see nothing except the camera, the cameraman, and a faint blue flicker where television receivers translated her picture onto screens.

Finally, Merchand said, "We'll let you know in a week or so. Thank you, Miss Dayton."

The stage lights went out, and Patricia blinked in relief. Derrick Merchand had already left the room, and the other members of the board were gathering their things and preparing to do the same. She glanced at each of them but couldn't tell whether or not she'd been approved. And she still didn't know if she had to sell Rose's cottage. A couple of years ago she had received an offer, but she had turned it down. She'd had no desperate need to sell it then. Even though nearly four years had passed since she had visited the island, she didn't want to sell the little house. She and her parents had spent many happy times there with Aunt Rose.

Rebecca Cloud met Patricia at the door to the apartment they shared. "Did you get the job?" she asked eagerly.

"I won't know for a week or longer."

"How did they act? Could you tell by what they said? Did Mr. Merchand sound like he wanted you?"

She wished he had. "If I put everything he said in my diary, I wouldn't fill a page. All he did was give orders: 'Say something'." she said in imitation. "'Take down your hair. Take off your jacket. We'll let you know in a week or so.'" She shrugged and smiled at her roommate. "In other words, don't call us, we'll call you."

"What about the atmosphere? Surely there were some kind of vibes."

"None that I noticed. I was blinded by lights most of the time so I couldn't see anything. I don't know if anyone smiled or scowled. When the session was over and they were leaving, a couple of the board members said thank you. Mr. Merchand was already gone. That's it."

"But you don't know you didn't get the contract."

"Correct." She tossed her purse onto the couch. "So I have to visit Aunt Rose's cottage this week. Why don't you come with me?"

"I would if I could, I'd love to get out of this blizzard cold. but there are three auditions I want to hit next week." She grinned. "And I don't know what Macy's would do without my help."

"You work harder at show business than you do at your job, Beck."

"Are you kidding? Show biz isn't work—it's a labor of love."

"It's a good thing Morris feels the same way or he'd never have got you to agree to marry him—even though you're crazy about him."

"I wish you were crazy about someone."

"Wish on. I'm not." Patricia took off her coat and went to hang it in the entry closet.

"Just because Bart was terrible doesn't mean all men are."

"Once burned, twice shy," Pat said.

"I wish you'd date someone."

"I do date someone. I date a lot."

"Not seriously. You never date the same man more than twice. It's been almost two years since Bart. You ought to be over him by now."

"I *am* over him. That didn't take long."

"You aren't over the effect."

She darted a quick glance at her curly-headed roommate. She had told Rebecca about her fantasies filtering into ordinary situations and knew that was what she was referring to. "I'm working on it," she said.

"A man would help. Pat, give someone else a chance."

"I will when I feel like it, but right now I don't even want to talk about it. I have to pack for my trip." She smiled. "*And* get ready for a date. I'm going out with Dudley Randolph tonight."

"Dudley? Who's Dudley?"

"A male model from the agency. They thought it would be good PR if we were seen together."

"*They* thought."

"Yes, they did. And, unlike you, who are free to do whatever you please, I do what they say. Are you going out with Morris tonight?"

"Yes. Pat, listen, I really am worried about you."

"Don't worry. Worry never helped anything or anybody. I think that's a direct quote from you. But thanks for caring. Want the shower first? Or shall I?"

"I've already bathed."

"Good. Then I can escape your matchmaker ten-
dencies under the spray." She patted the shorter girl
on the head as she went by. "Better get dressed for
Morris."

As Patricia showered she thought about Becky's concern. Many men had told Pat they loved her, had told
her she was beautiful, had said they couldn't live without her, but after her awakening by Bart, she hadn't
believed anyone's declarations. Becky had reason to be
worried.

But Patricia's mother didn't worry. Martha was a
die-hard optimist. For five years—ever since Patricia
turned twenty-one—she'd been telling her daughter
Mr. Right would come along and that everything would
be wonderful. Her expectations weren't dreams—she
believed them. But then, she'd found Parnell, and they
lived in a world filled with love and contentment and
happiness. They never wanted or needed anything or
anyone except each other. They loved their daughter.
but Patricia knew it was as much because she was a
physical result of their love as for anything. She sighed.
Their total affection for each other was something to
envy.

"Hey! I'm going," Becky shouted.

Patricia stuck her head around her bedroom door to
see Becky dwarfed by tall, gangly Morris. "Have a good
time, you two."

"Will do."

When Dudley came in a few minutes later, Pat was
dressed and waiting. The evening turned out to be a
flop, and Dudley turned out to be a dud. All he wanted
to talk about was himself: which side of his face photographed better, the jobs he'd had, some damn-fool
photographers he'd worked with. Patricia was re-

minded of what Derrick Merchand had said: he'd never known a model who didn't enjoy talking about the work and himself. Dudley was certainly like that, and more than once Pat caught herself drifting into fantasy to escape his emotional chatter.

Chapter Two

Patricia rented a car at the Tampa airport and drove south. She stopped at a supermarket and stocked up on everything she thought she might need. A butane stove was at the cottage, and she'd have to use candles and kerosene lamps because there was no electricity. She would have no television or radio unless she got battery-operated ones. She considered getting a small portable radio, and rejected the idea. She wanted to be completely cut off from civilization. And at Rose's cottage she would be, for it was the only house on Otter Key, off Florida's west coast. The little island was barely within sight of the mainland, and it wasn't accessible by car, there wasn't a ferry, and there wasn't a landing strip. The only way to get there was to have a boat or hire one to take you. She was glad. The last thing she wanted was a lot of tourists. She wanted time to think. She had to try to get herself straight and learn to live with what the world had to offer—not escape into dreams. She was determined to keep from sliding into fantasy for the entire week.

South of Sarasota, she turned right onto a long, curving two-lane road that led through salt flats to Bubba Lander's boat dock. Bubba looked exactly the same as he had the last time she'd seen him. That could have been the same chewed cigar he clenched between his teeth, the same grayed T-shirt over his rather large stomach.

"Patricia Dayton," he said. "Long time no see." He glanced into the backseat of her car. "Where're your folks?"

"They didn't come this time."

"You going out to Otter Key?"

"I thought I would for a little while."

"You're gonna be mighty lonely. Ain't no campers there that I know of. Place has been deserted all year except for maybe boaters who stopped for a picnic. Unless—" He paused. "No. Never mind."

"Unless what?" Patricia asked. He took his cigar out of his mouth but put it back before he spoke. "Rose's place ain't the only one out there anymore. There's a new house. Put up last year."

"Someone lives there?"

"Not lives there. Comes once in a while. But ain't no one there now so far as I know. I ain't seen hide nor hair of anyone. Bought up the rest of the island, they did, and built as far away from Rose's house as they could get and still build on dry land." He chuckled around the cigar butt. "Guess they're as antisocial as your aunt Rose was. They even wanted to buy up that bit of yours, so I told 'em who owned it. Did they get in touch?"

So that was why she'd gotten the offer. "Yes. A buyer called, but I turned the offer down. I may change my mind, though."

Bubba helped her load her things into the boat. "What you got in here? Rocks?" he asked as he carried one box for her.

"Books." She'd brought at least a dozen she'd been meaning to read and simply hadn't found the time. Now she would. With no TV, no radio, no telephone, and no company, she'd have time for reading. And sleeping. And thinking.

Bubba started the engine for her. "See you when I see you," he called.

She waved at him and pointed the nose of her boat toward the lift of land on the horizon. The water of the Gulf was calm today; scarcely a wave rippled on the surface, which reflected fleecy, flat-bottomed clouds. The fresh salt air gave her a heady feeling. She felt as if the closed-room air she'd breathed for the past months had cleared from her lungs, and the near frostbite she had suffered when she had gone outside in the frigid New York winter had melted in the balmy over-seventy degree temperature. She felt free and easy—more so than she'd felt in a long time.

Halfway to the Key a couple of bottle-nosed dolphins broke the surface a hundred yards from her boat. As they breathed, water sprayed in tiny droplets from their blowholes and made a hint of rainbow in the air before they submerged to come back up and repeat the process. She became engrossed with watching them and got off course. But that didn't matter, the island was more distinct and nothing was in her way. No other boats were in sight. She could go in circles if she wished, chase the porpoises if she felt like it. In a burst of free spirit she did just that. She guided the boat in a circle, then took off after the dolphins. They disappeared and she was sorry she had frightened them. She slowed, hoping the animals would appear again, but she didn't see them or any motion in the sea that would indicate they were still around.

A high-pitched sound, a near imitation of human laughter, came from the starboard. She glanced to see one of the porpoises slap his tail at her as he went under. The other leaped out of the water and gyrated to land with a massive splash before it, too, vanished. Then they surfaced together to look at her.

"Oh, you!" she shouted. She laughed with them before they disappeared again, this time for good.

She took another sighting of the island and aimed for the southern tip. The island was less than a mile long and was scarcely over a quarter of a mile wide at its widest point, and she had claim to a half acre of it; all the rest belonged to the owners of the new house. She hoped whoever owned the new place stayed away. If she needed company, she could go talk to Bubba.

Patricia laughed at herself. She was beginning to think like a recluse. Just because she was disenchanted with the world didn't mean everyone in it was bad.

As she drew nearer the island she could see shades of green and beige and gold. The short ramshackle dock in front of Rose's cottage was the only sign of civilization. She looked along the shoreline and could see no indication of the new house Bubba said had been built, and the trees seemed to be as thick as she remembered. She was relieved the land on the northern end hadn't been stripped.

She cut the motor, glided the last few yards to the dock, and tied the boat. Though she looked frail with her slender model's build, her soft skin and gentle roundness covered strong muscle and sinew. She managed everything—including the box of books—and when the boat was empty, she clambered onto the dock.

The cottage was deserted-looking: Rose's garden had

been neglected for years and was completely overrun, the clapboards were warped, and some of the screens looked in need of replacement. She'd bring screens and work on them the next time she came—if there were a next time. She might have to sell the house. She shook the thought away. She didn't know for certain she had to sell; she could get the Merchand contract.

Inside, the house smelled dusty and dank. Patricia began to open windows and paused at one of them to savor the absence of noise. There were no automobile engines or horns; there were no voices except those of birds and insects and small tree frogs. Occasionally a mullet jumped from the water and landed with a slap. The rustle of pine needles in the gentle breeze gave soft music, and the cadence of the almost nonexistent surf underlay the peaceful sound. She was glad she hadn't succumbed and brought a radio, as she'd have turned it on and lost the tranquillity of the sounds of nature. As the thought crossed her mind the hum of a distant plane came to her. She smiled. Well, she couldn't expect the entire world to stop living just because she wanted peace and quiet.

She went to work, but it was late afternoon before she had everything stowed in its proper place. She made a coldcut sandwich for dinner because she didn't want to bother with checking the stove to see if it worked properly. Tomorrow would be soon enough for that, she thought. She pulled a cold drink from the ice chest, popped the top, and washed down her meager meal.

By the time she was finished dusk was edging the day, but there was still enough light to allow a walk. She left the cabin by the back door and followed a path that led north through a grove of pine and oak trees, turned sharply, and came out on the seaward side to give a vast, uninterrupted view of the Gulf. A glorious sunset, with the sun nesting on the vibrating rim of water and spreading feathered fingers of colored clouds to right and left, was before her. Even the water picked up the rosy hue. She sat to lean against a tree and watch the splendor.

She hadn't been there long when she saw a man on the beach. He was a dark shape in the gray-blue-gold of fading light. He was fishing, wading in water about ankle deep. Once in a while he paused and cast into the depths offshore, reeled in, and then moved a little more in her direction. As far as she could tell, he hadn't a stitch on.

Slowly Pat stood, sliding her back against the tree, afraid to move suddenly or make any noise for fear he would hear her. The bark of the tree was rough on the bare skin between her halter and her shorts, sleepy bird cries and the gentle lap from undulations of the Gulf on the sandy shore were the only sounds she could hear, the tangy scent of pine trees mingled with clean fresh salt, and, unexpectedly, she craved the taste of that man's mouth on hers.

She moved from the tree. The man turned as if he'd seen movement, and she stopped. What was she doing? She stayed frozen, centered against the sheltering darkness of a background of trees, and watched him. He was gorgeous. His shoulders were broad and tapered to a trim waist and slim hips. His legs were long and wonderfully shaped. And he was as naked as on the day he had been born. He reminded her of the man in her fantasy. Her lips parted and her tongue slipped out to dampen them, but that was the only movement she made.

The man let his gaze search the woods for a moment, then with an almost invisible shrug he went back to fishing. Pat let her breath out slowly, and only then did she realize she had been holding it. He cast again and reeled in. As far as she could tell he'd had no luck at all. She smiled as she wondered where he would put his catch if he did get lucky.

She wanted to lean against the tree again so she would be more comfortable, but she was afraid if she moved she would be noticed, so she stayed where she was. The fisherman kept on until he was directly in front of her—not fifty feet away. The light was almost gone before he reeled in for the last time and, at a much faster clip than he'd come down it, went along the beach toward the north. She wanted to run after him, but she managed to contain herself.

Bubba must have been wrong; someone was staying in the new house. Or was the man a casual visitor to the island? She wondered whether he'd come from a boat or was staying in the house, sharing the island with her.

Certainly he was arrogant and self-assured, confident no one would mind seeing him run around as bare as Robinson Crusoe. Or was that Friday? Maybe he simply didn't care. He was built well enough to be proud of himself. She shook her head. There wasn't much to do along this stretch of coast, there were no restaurants, no bars, nothing. And when she had come across to the island, she hadn't seen a soul. He probably just didn't expect anyone.

She could be naked too, for all the world cared. The man had looked directly at her and hadn't seen her, and she had on a top that was lighter than her skin. No one would know or care if she stripped, so she did, and felt wickedly sensuous with the soft breeze playing on her skin. He had the right idea, that man with patience and nothing else to show for his fishing efforts.

A trace of early starlight, barely enough to let her make out the path to the cottage, deserted her when she went indoors. She should have left a light burning so she wouldn't have to search for matches in the dark, she admonished herself. She would next time. Suprised at herself, she realized she had made a decision to return the next evening to see if the man would be back. But he was the first man who had interested her even slightly since she had begun to fantasize. He had been beautiful and he had reminded her of her fantasy lover. If she'd had the courage to touch him, maybe that would have helped dispel her increasing tendency to drop into a dreamworld at the least provocation.

She lit a kerosene lamp, showered, then went to bed. She had been sleeping nude for years, and since she had taken her clothes off up the beach, she hadn't put more on. That in itself gave her a greater sense of freedom than did being away from work.

As she twisted the wick of the lantern so it stuttered out, she tried to recall when she'd taken a break from work the last time. It seemed like never. And it certainly hadn't been since she had met Bart.

The memory of Bart made her shudder. Bartholomew was a tall, attractive man with a strong nose and crystal blue eyes, but the crystalline character had nothing to do with color—it had to do with the cool, unfuzzy, and calculating way he looked at things. His mouth was sensuous and the words that came from it were persuasive. He seemed to know all the answers, and she had been young and sure of none—and he had taken her under his wing.

Pat hadn't been away from the protective shells of

family, home, college, and friends much more than three months. She had made stops at agencies and doled out portfolios as if they were free brochures from a charity group, but nothing had happened. She had managed to keep herself fed and sheltered and somewhat clothed by working in the accessory department of a store. That was where Bart had found her.

Shortly afterward, as if magic existed, doors began opening for her, and within a few months she started to be in demand as a model. She made money and Bart told her how to spend it. She had never had much money and it was easy to let the cash drift through her fingers as quickly as he suggested ways for it to go. At that time she thought he loved her—he told her he did. Why else would someone do so much for someone else? she had wondered.

Pat felt gratitude toward him and felt she owed him something, and she offered him love. She believed she loved him, thought someday they'd get married. He helped her set up charge accounts and he helped her fill them to bursting, and she let him. She didn't know then that he was a panderer, living off women, good at nothing except knowing the right people.

When Patricia mentioned money to him and spoke of how bills were piling up in her name, he didn't listen. She'd get more money, he told her. And she did, but not nearly enough to clear up debts that had grown unbelievably. Bart had access to her cards and he used them at will. Charges were listed for things she had never seen, would never see. If she asked about them, he gave her a runaround story about public relations, oiling the right hinge, putting money where it would do the most good. He opened accounts at stores she had never been to—didn't even know existed—and she began to receive bills from them as well. He used her name, built her up in the eyes of proprietors as being more successful than she ever hoped to be, exercised his suave ability to con. And nearly every evening he insisted they go to dinner, to a show, to a concert—somewhere to be seen by the right people. Those outings cost money. Her money.

A time came when she needed something from one of the stores. It was a small item—night cream—but she hadn't been allowed to charge it. She'd exceeded her limit, they said. How could that have been? Her limit was for thousands of dollars.

Bart had been busy.

When she faced him with a record of his charges, he tried to placate her, but she was beyond the placating stage. He said he would begin paying the bills and help her out. He never had, never would, never planned to do so.

Patricia worked every day, but she couldn't make a dent in her debts because interest charges increased them faster than she could decrease them. She became exhausted by the never-ending work, the constant late nights, the unpayed bills. Then she learned Bart was married. He had been separated from his wife for years, he said; their marriage was over. She still thought they would get married after he was divorced, but every time she mentioned it, he stalled.

One evening Bart had come to the apartment and seen her methodically feeding one credit card after another into the fire. She asked for those he had, but he wouldn't give them to her. He told her they would have nothing to fall back on if she got rid of them. Pat figured they had done enough falling back to last a lifetime and she wanted to stop the avalanche. He distracted her with studied charm and with plans he had made for them to get married. He had never been so positive about their wedding before, and she forgot about the cards—until the next day when the reality of the situation hit her with force again. She wrote a letter to each of the stores, restaurants, clubs—whatever—to say she would not be responsible for any more expenses registered to her account.

When Bart discovered what she had done, he was furious. He had been made to look foolish and ridiculous. How could she have done it to him? She tried to explain that none of the bills had diminished during the last months, though she'd been working steadily and had been earning high pay, and that something had to be done.

Bart was around only a short time longer. Pat was no longer so pliable, so easy to con, and he left, saying she was selfish and self-centered and wasn't worth his time. He couldn't close the doors he had opened for her because she was good at what she did, but he would have if he could have.

Patricia had moved into the smaller apartment she now shared with Rebecca and had steadily chipped away at the bills, but the interest rates kept them high and she had been able to wipe out only the smallest ones. Then her mother had gotten sick. For the first year Parnell had been able to handle the expenses, but after Martha had her operations, financial matters had got out of hand for her parents too. He had asked Pat for help. She couldn't turn down her parents—she loved them. If she hadn't been so naive and trusting she never would have got into the fix she was in. She had never loved Bart. She had been infatuated with him, had reveled in the attention he paid her when they met, had believed the compliments he had heaped on her.

However, Bart had never made her feel like a woman, not a real woman, one who was warm, capable, and cherished. He had behaved more as if she were a vassal whose duty was to her master. Patricia had known something was missing, but she hadn't known what it was because Bart was so fluent with persuasion. Any time she questioned him or doubted him, he was there with a reminder of how much he had done for her, how much she owed him, how beautiful she was, and how he needed her. She had had no experience with anyone like him, and he had manipulated her— started her on her way, he said. She found out later that she would have got a start anyway if she had been patient.

After she had broken up with Bart, her outlook on people was jaded. It was no wonder she had built a world to hide in. In order to find someone she could trust, someone who loved her for herself, someone she could love, she had created a world where such a person existed. Her dream man was fabulous, and there were no bills, and no one took advantage of her.

But she couldn't live in a fantasy. She had to face life. And she could. If she got the Merchand contract, she'd get a healthy advance. If she didn't, she could sell the cottage. Things weren't totally hopeless. She at least had hope.

Chapter Three

Patricia spent the day in idleness. She began reading one of her books. but it didn't hold her attention because she kept remembering the man on the beach. He was a free spirit, a man who didn't feel shame about the human body, and she would probably never see him again. With such poor results, who would go fishing two nights in a row? But her thoughts of him were as pointless as her fantasies; she was making the fisherman into a fantasy.

"It was me," the dream lover said. "I didn't want to frighten you away; you weren't expecting to see me." Her fantasy slid in on her so smoothly, she was scarcely aware of a change. "I love you, Patricia. I'll never do anything to hurt you. I'll never lie to you." He came nearer, but she couldn't see his face. Had she ever been able to? What color were his eyes? she wondered. "Come with me." he said.

"No," she said aloud, and loudly. She wasn't going to do this! she told herself. One of the main reasons she was on Otter Key was to make herself stop dreaming unless she needed it for work.

She got up from her lawn chair and went to the shore. The waves were higher today and the throb of surf was more distinct. A couple of shrimp boats, far out, hazed with the distance, were aiming for port. Day was almost gone.

Since she had gotten here, she'd had nothing warm to eat. She still didn't want to go to the trouble, but knew she should. She should have checked the stove earlier. She had done nothing but diddle away the day and now felt guilty, and at the same time knew she shouldn't feel that way—she deserved a few days of inactivity and irresponsibility. But not eating was carrying idleness too far.

After she got the stove going, Pat prepared a simple meal and ate. She dawdled, taking as much time as she reasonably could, and afterward she washed the dishes and pans, handling them as though they were made of priceless porcelain. She wasn't going to let herself go to the beach again. Her immediate interest in a total stranger was as peculiar as was her tendency to drop into dream.

Her bath didn't take long. After she dried, she was tempted again to go look for the fisherman, so she got back into the shower and washed her hair. That didn't take long either. She put on shorts, and a blouse, which she tied into a midriff. The sun was still up, and though it was only a finger width above the horizon, it might furnish enough heat to help dry her hair. She went to sit on a fallen log near the water. Behind some trees to her right the sun was setting. The sunset was going to be as lovely as the one the day before, but she wouldn't go back to the west shore to watch it. She took off her sandals and waded into the easy surf and watched the sea change colors with the spreading molten glow from the sun.

It was as silly to stay away as it was to go, she thought.

She left her sandals behind and half-walked, half-ran along the path to the turn and the gap in the trees. The fisherman wasn't on the beach, and she couldn't stop a catch of disappointment. She hadn't come to see him, she told herself, she'd come to watch the sun go down.

The sunset was more glorious today than yesterday. It was wider and deeper, with more diffused and tangled tints: red, orange, pink, purple, yellow, lavender. If anyone wore such a combination of colors, no one would see who was in the clothes because the outfit would be too magnificent. Slowly and inexorably the sun vanished behind the rim of the world until nothing but a scarlet dab of an arc remained at the center of radiance. That fleck went with a quick swallow of greedy earth and only mingled colors remained. She could almost feel herself spinning backward at unimaginable speeds, rotating away from the sun.

Pat left the shelter of trees and sauntered toward the surf, looking north along the shore as far as the island reached—and it was empty. She felt lonely, and knew the feeling was foolish.

She picked up a bit of clam shell, absently dusted damp sand from it, then tossed it into the sea. He wasn't going to come, she knew. Suddenly she was tired. The stress and fatigue that had been building up hit her and her shoulders slumped. That was why they sagged. Surely it wasn't because of disappointment.

She had no reason to stay longer—the sun was gone. Slowly, with her head down so she could watch where she stepped, she started back the way she had come. It was already too dark to see clearly, and she'd come without shoes. Though the path was covered with pine needles, pine cones sprinkled the way, and she didn't relish the idea of one of the spiny things sticking her foot.

"You came back," he said. His voice was deep and warm and low and rich.

She glanced up. He was in the shadows, leaning against the tree where she'd been the evening before. A thrill of excitement touched her, a thrill of almost recognition. "Yes," she said.

"I saw you looking along the shore. I was there earlier. I wasn't sure you'd come."

"I did."

He took a couple of steps toward her. He had on bathing trunks this time. "Why are you here?"

"I—" She couldn't tell him she had come to see him. But in the faded light she couldn't see him. His face was just an area scarcely paler than his hair and the shadows of the trees around and behind him. His skin had the look of burned copper. For a second his eyes caught a tardy beam of reflected sunlight and seemed golden, and she wondered if gold was their real color or if that was only an effect caused by light.

"What color are your eyes?" she asked.

"Hazel. Why?"

"I wondered."

He chuckled. "Are you real?"

That was a question she could have asked. "Yes," she said. "Very."

He came closer, and she could see darkness like a shadow on his chest.

"No, you aren't," he said. "You're a dryad or a naiad who appears at dusk."

"No."

"Who are you?"

She started to tell him, then changed her mind. "No names."

He laughed again, softly. "You're a statue come to life, that's what you are. No flesh-and-blood woman could have stayed as still as you did last night. I thought you were a statue then—a marble statue someone had left under the trees."

"You saw me?"

"I'm not sure. I saw something." He came nearer, and she could sense the rise and fall of his chest as he breathed. She could smell the aroma of him: salty and warm, with a hint of Coppertone. His arm lifted and a finger gently touched her throat above the dip between it and her collarbone. The touch moved to the side and up to stop beneath her ear, where her pulse had begun to pound more rapidly. "You're real, all right," he said.

"Are you?" Her hand went to spread on his chest, and the wiry feel of hair was vital in her palm. She jerked away.

Gently his hand touched her wrist and slid upward until it met the sleeve of her blouse, made the jump to bare skin, and moved to grasp the nape of her neck and draw her to him. His head lowered until his lips brushed hers softly.

"Oh," she said, all breath and no sound.

"Yes," he said. His other arm slipped around her waist to hold her near. His mouth came to hers and moved silkily and tenderly from side to side, up and down. She could feel his breath on her cheek, hear his inhalations, his exhalations. "Now," he whispered. His lips parted, took hers with them, and his tongue dipped into her mouth. He stroked her back, then buried his hands in her hair.

A thread of desire tickled low in her abdomen and traveled upward to envelop her brain, and she wanted to be closer to him than was physically possible. She melted against him, and her arms went to caress his back, to feel the muscles move beneath his skin, to hold him nearer. Her breath became short, and she answered the probing of his kiss with a hunger she hadn't known she owned. She wanted nothing more than to have him then and there, in the deepening dark of evening, on the soft and pungent pine.

He murmured deep in his throat, drew slightly away, and put his arms over hers, capturing them beneath his, making her reach around his waist. Sinuously his hands slid down to grasp her hips, and that lifted her need for him even higher. He traced the shape of her lips with his tongue, and another, heavier, sound came from him, and he closed on her mouth again, his tongue demanding her response. He loosened the knot in her shirt and unfastened the button that kept it shut, then his hand went inside and tested, lifting lightly, feeling the weight of her breast, tracing the roundness of it, before he clasped, holding all of it within his fingers. His other hand went to cradle her other breast as his mouth left hers and trailed soft nuzzles along the side of her neck to the hollow of her throat, then his lips and hand fought for possession of her breast. His mouth won, and the defeated hand went to hold her hip. As if one war hadn't been enough, his mouth moved to fight away the other hand and win. His lips came to hers again and his hands went under her blouse in back to pull her against his chest. "I want you," he said. "God, I want you." He drew her with him toward the ground. "Come down here with me. I want to make love to you."

Every one of her nerves was tuned to vitality, and her brain was addled with a strange electricity. She'd never felt so alive, had never been so conscious of the fibers of her being.

He was already kneeling. His hands were on her, sending surges of warmth wherever they touched, and his mouth was a center to her heat as the sun had been the focal point of sunset. But as the soft sting of pine needles touched her back, truth touched her mind. "No," she said so softly, the word could have been the breath of wind in a tree or the brush of water on the sand. She held his face, but she couldn't see him: he was a dark silhouette against the deep gray of sky. Who was he? She couldn't make love with a man she couldn't see. "No," she said.

"This could never happen again," he said. "Love me." His mouth moved to take her breast again as he began to unfasten her shorts. "Wait," she said. "Stop. Who are you?"

"No names, remember? No past, no present, no future."

"No." She grabbed his head to hold him away.

"We'll never have another chance at this, I have to leave. I won't be here tomorrow."

"I can't."

"What do you mean, you can't? A minute ago you could."

"But I didn't know—"

His mouth came down on hers again, persuasively, urging her to open to him. She felt herself submerging, going down to the power of his sensuality, drifting to his lure. Then her hands were on his chest, pushing him. "I didn't know what I was doing," she said, nearly panicked.

"But you spied on me last night, and you came back this evening looking for me."

"No!" she shouted, still pushing him away. "You don't understand."

"You're right. I *don't* understand." He removed himself from her so abruptly, her hands had no chance to follow, and she was left holding only the memory of his shape.

The warm Florida air touched her flesh like winter's draft, but she was thankful he had stopped. She wouldn't have been able to make him quit. She couldn't blame him for trying, as she'd held him and kissed him as if she knew him and loved him and wanted him. "I don't know you," she said weakly, knowing that was no excuse.

"I don't know you either. What difference does that make? This was a wild and wonderful chance meeting, and we wanted each other." He bent toward her and his lips touched hers, teasing and stirring. "Can you tell me you don't want me?" he whispered against her. "Can you?" His hand cupped her breast and his mouth took hers with a mind-and-body-filling heat.

"Please, don't." She was almost unable to speak, and her hands as they pushed him had little strength. "Please."

"I won't." His voice sounded resigned, and he let go of her and sat up. "Why did you come to me if you didn't want to make love to me?"

"I came to see the sunset. I live here."

"No one lives here."

"I do. I have a cottage on the end of the island." A new apprehension hit her. If he was the owner of the new house, she didn't know what she would do—she would be vastly embarrassed to see this man again. "Do you live here?"

He was silent for a moment. "No, I don't."

She breathed a sigh of relief. "I'm sorry about letting you think what you thought," she said, "about my—my motivations."

"I'm sorry too." He stood, but he was between her and the backdrop of sea and sky, and she could see nothing other than the outline of his body. "How long will you be staying on the island?" he asked. "I may get a chance to come back."

"Not long. And don't come back."

"You can't tell me to do or not do that." His voice changed, grew softer and deeper. He bent swiftly, drew her to her feet, and kissed her lips as if he owned them. "I'll see you again. That's a promise." He turned and disappeared under the darkness of trees.

She shivered in the air, which seemed cold and empty without him. She stuffed the tails of her blouse into the band of her shorts, thinking that would help warm her. It didn't. She had escaped doing something impulsive, but she wasn't altogether sure she was glad she had.

Pat went along the path and was within sight of home before she realized that she hadn't lit a lantern this night either. And he would be gone tomorrow.

Maybe she should leave as well, she thought, she'd seen the cottage, but until Merchand made its decision, she didn't know whether or not she'd have to sell. She had bought her plane ticket and had rented a car and a boat, so it would be foolish of her to let the money she had spent go to waste. She had done enough of that in one lifetime to have lasted three. And it was cold up north.

The fisherman wouldn't come back. Even though she had told him where she lived, he wouldn't. Not even if she wished he would. And if he wouldn't be here, there was no reason for her not to stay.

For the rest of her time on the island she didn't venture away from the southern tip. Instead she read three of the books she'd brought, got a light golden tan, and didn't slip into fantasy once. Each time she felt she might, she got her dream lover mixed up with the man on the beach. She was curious about what the meeting under the pines might do to her ability to pull forth a proper expression for the camera. Would the man in her fantasy be the same? Or would he be replaced? Maybe the man on the beach would merge into her dreams only to make her fantasy more real, more difficult to escape.

Pat tried to analyze the difference between the two men. Had her fantasy lover been as tall as the fisherman? As broad? Had his skin been as tantalizing to touch? Had his kiss filled her with such instant desire? She couldn't judge. It seemed the fisherman was everything her dream lover had been. That was why she had gone so easily into his arms. Now what the figment of her imagination lacked she could fill in with memories of the other. He had hazel eyes, he said. But she hadn't seen them any more than she'd seen the eyes of her fantasy lover. She had no idea how either of them looked. Their shape, she knew; how they felt, she knew that, all right.

Chapter Four

Patricia was sure her blood had thinned during her short visit in the warm climate for, despite the wool coat she had on, the cold reached to the center of her bones. It would take awhile for her to adjust to winter again.

Becky wasn't home, so she unpacked and looked at her mail: nothing from Merchand. She hadn't really expected anything; she'd been gone scarcely a week.

When Rebecca came in, her cheeks were red from the cold and fresh snowflakes clung to her scarf and the shoulders of her coat. The first thing she wanted to know was if Patricia had found a man. Pat had known she would ask and was prepared for the question, but she couldn't stop her blush as she recalled her passionate gropings with the man on the beach.

"You know the island is deserted, Beck," she said, looking away. "Where would I have found a man? Hiding under a scallop shell?"

"You could have crossed to the mainland, gone to Tampa or Sarasota for a break." She grinned. "A rich tycoon in a yacht could have shipwrecked on your shore."

Pat laughed. "You're as bad a dreamer as I am."

"Stranger things have happened." Becky grew serious. "Look, dear roommate of mine, if you don't see people, how are you going to find out if such a person as you wish existed really does? You aren't totally unique—everyone has a dream man. Some people just find them more easily than others, but if you don't look, you'll never know."

"I promise you'll be the first person I tell if I ever do find him." She felt guilty saying that when she didn't even intend to tell about the man she'd been with for those few brilliant moments. "Did anyone call?"

"Dudley. What's with him? His voice sounded funny."

"He's trying to develop a British accent. He thinks it'll give him a more cosmopolitan air."

"It makes him sound weird. He wanted to go out with you again."

"He can go ahead and want."

"Not *the* man, huh?"

"Far from it in every sense."

Becky shook her coat and went to hang it in the closet. Over her shoulder she said casually, "I'm going out with Morris tonight, and I could get him to bring a friend." She spun to face Pat. "Why don't you let him this time?"

"Good grief, Beck, I just got back from a trip. I haven't had time to unwind yet. I'm still tense." She gave a half-smile. "And I'm not sure I'll be able to relax until I hear from Merchand about the job either."

"You'll get the contract," Becky said. "They'd be crazy to pass you up."

"Sure. The roommates of the other two girls are probably telling them the same thing."

"Yep, but those girls are wrong. I'm not. You'll see."

Becky's confidence in Pat's eventual success didn't help. Pat was almost afraid to leave the apartment. Merchand hadn't said how she'd be notified, but if the news came by telephone, she didn't want to miss it. Even though she had an answering machine, she wanted to know instantly and not hear a tinny recorded voice tell her sorry, and she rushed to get the mail each time it came.

When a message did come, it was by phone, asking her to make another appearance. This time the other girls would be there; some of the board members wanted to compare the choices side by side. Derrick Merchand wanted to compare them, Pat thought. His word was law at Merchand Corporation.

Each of the applicants would accent her most desirable feature, so Pat studied herself, trying to decide what hers was. She was kind of all-over okay: no single attribute was outstanding. Her eyes were wide and blue and had good lashes and well-shaped brows, her nose was neat and straight, her mouth was a mouth—nicely shaped, but with no special appeal. Hair could be any color, but the texture and natural shade of hers was as good as she could imagine it: reddish-brown. A common shade, brown. Ordinary.

She took off her clothes and inspected her body. Her breasts weren't large, but they were uplifted and firm. She felt a tendril of desire as she recalled the fisherman holding them. She touched them, but she couldn't cover them as completely as he had. Her hands slipped past her waist to caress her hips the way he had.

Lord, she *was* a dreamer.

She glanced at herself and saw an expression of leashed concupiscence. That was her best feature—that look. No wonder she'd needed fantasy. That look was definitely female, base female, the way men wanted women to feel. It was an on-the-brink-of-capitulating expression; not an outright I'm-yours-if-you-want-me look, but an if-you-say-the-right-things-I-don't-think-I-can-resist look. She'd have to play up that quality. If she wanted the Merchand contract, she'd have to dip into fantasy. She hadn't during the last session because she had been too busy following directions and trying to hold products so the camera could read the words.

Then she saw her reflection return to pretty, healthy, normal Patricia Dayton. She chose a pastel pink silk dress that brought out the highlights in her hair and enhanced the warm flesh tones of her skin. She was glad she hadn't gone too far on Otter Key and got sun-burned. The dress had a high neckline and was but-toned in front, but by leaving the top two buttons undone she gave the hint that more was available be-neath if someone wanted to take the necessary effort to discover it. She hated to cover her dress with her heavy coat—it was old and ugly—but it was the only one she had and if she didn't wear it, she'd freeze to death.

Pat caught a taxi, but not two blocks from her apart-ment they ran into a traffic jam. She looked at her watch and wasn't terribly disturbed; plenty of time was allowed for such contingencies. But after a few minutes of not moving at all, she began to be concerned. Cars were piled up behind them and in front of them. The cab could do nothing but sit patiently and wait for things to clear. She was about to say something to the driver when the car inched forward a trace, then darted ahead a couple of car lengths, and she was sure the street had been unclogged. She glanced at her watch again and saw she could still be punctual. But the taxi stopped again. Sitting forward to look through the windshield at what had stopped them, all she could see was the rear ends of cars stretching in staggered lines in front of her. Behind was another mass with headlights and grills in a mélange of varied angles.

"What's wrong?" she asked the driver.

"How should I know?" he said and shrugged. "New York."

She glanced at her watch nervously. If she was on the way now, and going at a normal pace, she'd make it on time. She looked for a subway entrance. If she caught an express, maybe she wouldn't be too late. She spied one, and the taxi started. This time they made it three blocks before they were forced to another halt.

"Oh, fantastic," she said in irritation. "I'm going to be late for an appointment."

"Isn't everybody?"

Patricia wanted to cry. What a wonderful way to make a good impression! Her second time at Merchand headquarters, and she drags in late as if she doesn't need or want the job. "I've _got_ to get there."

The driver turned in his seat to look at her disdainfully. "You can walk, lady. I'm doing all I can."

"Where's the subway?"

"Couple of blocks over." He stuck his hand over the seat back for the fare.

She looked out at the slush and ice piled along the sidewalks, at the tiny flakes of snow mixed with small particles of sleet. At that moment she was glad she'd decided to wear boots and carry her sandals. She'd have to walk two blocks, wait for the subway, then walk from the exit to the Merchand building.

"Are you going to get out?" the driver asked.

She took a deep breath and let it out in a puff. "No. This is probably as fast as any other mode of transportation." She leaned back and tried to relax, take it in stride, but she was as wired up as the Shea scoreboard. "At any rate," she said, "it's warmer in here than out there."

"Soon as we get out of this, I'll do my best, lady." Within a few minutes he saw a break ahead. "We got it."

She closed her eyes as he gunned the motor and headed for an opening that couldn't be wide enough. He got through without a screaming protest of metal on metal, and she looked back to see the space between a stalled garbage truck and a car parked on the side of the street and knew they couldn't have made it. But they had, and the cab was screeching corners and catching lights that were on their way to red. She got to Merchand's ten minutes late. She gave the driver a generous tip: he'd done his best. As she rushed into the building, she hoped Derrick Merchand was late, or hadn't planned a tight schedule. And she knew she'd blown it.

When she reached the outer office, the receptionist looked up at her. "You're late."

Patricia rolled her eyes. If anyone knew she was late, *she* did. "Traffic jam," she said.

"The others are already in."

"Oh, Lord." She started to hurry to the door, then remembered her shoes. "Oh, Lord," she said again, and dashed to a couch, sat down, and began to jerk at the straps that kept her boots on. She nearly broke a nail. That wouldn't help matters at all, she knew. She tried to calm down and be patient, but her fingers seemed all to have turned to thumbs. She used the toe of one boot to shove the other off, and slipped on her sandal. Worried and harried by the fate of delay, she bent over to fasten the shoe and heard a door open. What if the interview was already over? All they had to do was compare the three. She looked up. Derrick Merchand was in the doorway.

When Pat had glanced at him during the first interview, she'd known he was strikingly attractive, but she hadn't registered the absolute magnificence of him. And he had been sitting, so she hadn't known he was so tall or so broad. His dark gray suit fit him as if it had been molded to his form. The subtly patterned, muted tie was centered exactly in the throat of his white shirt. Not a strand of his too-long hair was out of place. His eyes, somewhere between green and brown, looked at her sternly.

"Miss Dayton?"

"Yes," she tried to say, but her lips moved with no sound.

His gaze didn't waver from her as he unfastened the button that kept his jacket closed, swept it back on either side, and planted his fists on his hips. The fit of his trousers told her that he knew the assets of his shape and that he wasn't ashamed to broadcast. "You decided to come," he said.

"I—I—" She wanted to explain about the traffic. "Did," she said. He was gorgeous, and she looked like a frump crouched over in her two-year-old wool coat with one sandal on and one fur-lined boot half off.

"Need some help?" he asked, raised an eyebrow, and nodded toward her feet.

"I can manage," she said and tried to force herself into some kind of composure. "Thank you."

She straightened, shoved off her coat, trying to make it invisible behind her. Then she bent to remove the boot. As she did she glanced at Merchand. His gaze had dropped to hover at the opening of her bodice, and she knew he could see a hint of shadow within and the gentle rise of flesh. She blushed lightly. But that was why she'd undone the top buttons, wasn't it? To lead the eye and the mind to curiosity about what was inside? Still, her head dipped farther than was necessary as she released the boot and drew on the other sandal. When she was shod, she rose, and the soft folds of the dress fell into place. She looked at him again. He still stood with his hands on his hips, and he was still studying her, all of her, but he seemed overly fascinated with her cleavage. Maybe she'd gone too far in her dress. She hadn't thought she was suggestive.

"Are you ready now?" he asked.

"Yes."

"We're waiting." Using the same deliberation with which he had undone it, he drew his jacket together and slipped the button into place.

Patricia wasn't sure she could walk, but she did, and at the last minute Merchand stepped out of her way and let her through the doorway first. The other two girls were on the platform, and she was sure, as she saw them, she had in no way been overly seductive in her outfit, because the brunette was voluptuous and sexy in a tight low-cut gown that showed the tops of generous breasts and the full curves of her hips; her face was as sensuous as her body. The honey-blond was fresh and young in a sporty outfit. The young look was fantastically popular—near infants were invading the field—so no doubt the blond girl would have a definite edge.

"Miss Dayton," Merchand said.

She glanced at him. He had stopped and was watching her study the other girls.

"Please join them," he said. "We have waited long enough."

As if his voice were the lash of a whip goading her, she took off—and nearly tripped over herself getting to the stand. Once there, she didn't know where to go. She looked toward the board members and was met with the same curtain of light that had prevented her seeing anything the last time.

"Miss Dayton." Merchand's voice came from where he'd been when she left him; he hadn't gone to his seat. She turned to see him but couldn't, and she was glad. She had been late. had behaved in a gauche manner, and was as confused as she had ever been. She would never get the job and she knew it.

"Would you please take the empty chair." His voice now came from the head of the table.

She gave up trying to see through the glare, drew herself proudly erect, walked sedately to the chair he indicated, and sat with as much dignity as she could muster.

There was silence for such a long time, she wondered what was going on. No doubt the board members were studying the three and comparing each to the other. She could hear the faint rustling of paper; someone was taking notes.

"Miss Dayton, could you give us an expression other than absolute panic? We don't want people to be terrified to buy Merchand products."

She flicked her eyes toward the room, saw nothing except light, and dropped into fantasy. Her dream lover was with her; she could almost touch him. "I've waited years to find you," he said as he caressed her cheek. "I love you, Patricia." His hand drifted to her throat, went lower to pause at the top fastened button of her dress. Her lips parted and her eyes nearly closed with anticipation as a rush of desire spread over her. "Come down here with me," he said. Suddenly, he became the man on the beach. She couldn't see his face, but she could smell his presence and feel the warmth of his touch.

"Ah," she said in mild protest.

"Now," he said.

If the man on the beach insisted on becoming part of her fantasy world, she could do little to stop him; she had more or less expected it anyway. His breath teased her lips before his mouth met hers. Methodically she removed the pins from her hair. She didn't want any confinement from the sea breeze, wanted to feel the swing of her hair caught by the flow of it. His fingers played on her face and her neck and her arms, tugged at the closed buttons as if encouraging her to unfasten one more, just one, so he could relish the sight, so he could more easily reach inside. Her hand went to stop him—or help him—she wasn't sure which.

"Would the three of you stand together toward the front of the platform," someone said. It wasn't Merchand.

Patricia half lost her fantasy as she moved. But he was just this side of the lights, waiting for her, a bit impatient at the delay. "You came to see me," he said. "This could never happen again. Let's make the most of it."

She shook her head, not certain whether the negative gesture was in denial of him or at her own restraining morals. "I love you," he said. "I've never loved anyone the way I love you."

It had been at herself that she shook her head. Her hand went again to the closed button, but enough of reality remained to stop her: the lights were vaguely there, the members of the board, Derrick Merchand. She didn't undo it.

"That'll be all," Merchand said. "Thank you. All of you."

The stage lights went off, and Patricia was staring into Derrick's eyes as if she'd known exactly where he was in the blind place behind the curtain of glare.

"Miss Frederick and Miss Land, I'd like a private interview with each of you," he said, but his gaze didn't move from Pat. She had to lower her eyes to avoid his stare. "Miss Dayton, I'll see you in my office now."

He had made his decision—that was obvious. And when she went to see him, he would tell her either good-bye and thanks for the trouble or that she had the job. She had no idea which.

When she looked up, he wasn't there. She didn't have the slightest idea where his office was or which way he'd gone. She looked around helplessly.

A slender man, topped with a shock of burnt-orange hair, touched her arm. "This way, Miss Dayton." He guided her past the upholstered chairs to a doorway in the rear of the room. They went through an intricate series of halls, entered at an ornate door, and went through an outer office to another door equally as splendid as the first. The man rapped and, without waiting for a response, opened the door and ushered her inside.

Merchand was seated behind a large and imposing desk that was crowded with books and papers. He had a telephone in one hand and was jotting on a legal pad with the other. He glanced up. "Thank you, Russell," he said, and went back to listening and writing. Russell left.

Patricia didn't know what to do. For a moment she stayed where she was, watching Merchand concentrate on his phone and his pad. He paid no attention to her, so she went to a chair in front of the desk and sat, crossed her legs, and looked around. The office was huge and had a plate glass window that gave a view of the skyline. Leather chairs were arranged casually in front of the window, and a low table was within reach of three of them. The room had been cleverly divided by the placement of furniture into a thoroughly businesslike area and a more relaxed informal corner. Other than the door through which she had entered, there were two others: one most likely led to a bathroom, the other was possibly an escape hatch for Merchand if he wanted to evade someone.

"You do have a delightful body," Merchand suddenly said as he hung up the phone.

The man on the beach had said that to her. Her gaze whipped to meet Merchand's. He was nonchalant and at ease, leaning back in his chair with his fingers steepled before his chest, his elbows resting on the arms of the chair. Why had she thought about the fisherman? Just because Merchand happened to use the same phrase the man had used meant nothing. A lot of men had said much the same thing to her. She did have a good body: slender, yes, and not voluptuous, but it was well proportioned and she moved gracefully. "Thank you," she said.

He watched her a moment with a hint of knowledge in his eyes; as if he knew more about her than he could know. "I'd like to offer you the job, Miss Dayton," he said in a businesslike manner as he straightened in his chair. "But there are certain amendments I'd like to have made in the contract. I won't dismiss the other two women until I'm sure you'll agree to the changes."

"Oh," she said, and her voice was high-pitched, not at all like the modulated tones she usually projected. The release from the tension of not knowing was immediate, and for a second she thought she might faint. Then she grinned. Her worries were over. She wouldn't have to sell Rose's cottage. She'd be able to get out from under her bills, pay off her mother's hospital debts, help her parents reestablish themselves. "Thank you," she said. "Wonderful!"

"The terms of the contract will be stringent."

"Okay. That's okay."

He was silent, thoughtful, and a muscle jumped in his jaw. "Perhaps you'd better reserve your decision until you read it. You might find some objections then."

She thought the contract would have to be dreadful to keep her from signing. "I'm sure it will be agreeable."

He continued to study her as he unfastened his jacket and slipped it from his shoulders, but he took his gaze off her as he stood to drape it over the back of his chair. He wandered to the window and tucked his hands into his hip pockets as he looked at the view. "You'll have to do everything I say," he said, and turned languidly to face her. "I'm afraid you'll feel more owned by me than hired."

If she accepted the contract, she knew she'd be expected to reflect the Merchand Corporation a hundred percent. There would be restrictions on what she wore and where she went, and she'd be allowed to use only Merchand cosmetics. "I'll read the contract," she said.

"We'll have a copy for you tomorrow. Two o'clock?"

"Fine." She got up and started to leave. She could scarcely wait to get home to tell Becky and call her folks.

"Miss Dayton!" he said as if she had broken a cardinal rule by leaving without his dismissal. Maybe she had.

Pat turned toward him. "Yes? Sorry."

"Your first name is Patricia, isn't it?"

He should know that; he had her application. "It is," she said.

"My name is Derrick Merchand."

She looked at him in confusion. Did he think she didn't know who he was? "I know," she said. She thought maybe he would tell her what she should call him if she did go to work for him. He didn't.

A smiled tugged at his lips but didn't succeed in destroying his serious expression entirely. "My, my," he said, and turned to look out the window once more. "I'll see you tomorrow at two, Patricia," he said.

"Yes." She didn't know whether to be formal and call him Mr. Merchand or call him by his first name as he had her. He was her boss—or soon would be—and she shouldn't use familiarity without permission. "Yes," she repeated, deciding not to call him anything. "I'll be on time. I'll leave home early."

"Do that." He didn't look at her again. "Ask my secretary to come in, would you?"

"Yes." She waited to see if he wanted to add anything, but he didn't.

In the outer office the carrot-topped young man was seated behind the desk. "Are you Mr. Merchand's secretary?" she asked.

"Yes."

"He wants to see you."

Russell was up and gone before she got to the door. And she had gone only a few steps, not knowing where she was headed because she'd arrived at the office from a circuitous route, when Russell came out the door behind her.

"This way, Miss Dayton," he said.

She followed him along a short hall and into the reception room, where the other applicants waited. She kept her face noncommittal. It was Merchand's duty and not hers to tell them who was first in line to represent his company. She felt sorry for the losers. She could have been one of the also-rans, and she would have felt like dying. But if she approved the contract, she had the job. She wanted to jump and shout.

Pat put on her coat, changed back into her snow boots, and got outside before her exuberance burst from her. "I got it!" she shouted. "I got the job!" Scarcely anyone looked at her. She whirled with her arms outstretched—and was lucky she didn't hit someone. "I got it, I got it, I got it!"

Chapter Five

Patricia was so excited, it was the next day before she calmed down. She had phoned her folks, who were happy at her success, and she'd told Rebecca, who, if anything, was more delighted than she. It was near time to dress for her two o'clock appointment before she could think clearly about the way Derrick Merchand had behaved the day before. He had said things in strange ways. She couldn't put her finger on anything definite, but his pauses had been weird, his phrasing a bit off kilter. Well, he was president and chairman of the board, and though he couldn't be over thirty-five, he had the right to be a trifle eccentric if he wanted to be.

She decided to get ready earlier than was necessary so she would have time to stop at the library and look up the company. Not because of Derrick, she told herself, but because she'd be working for him—for his company—and she ought to be more knowledgeable.

Patricia was as careful in choosing what to wear today as she had been yesterday. She didn't want to look overpowering or smug, but she didn't want to seem too casual, as if she didn't care now that she had been offered the contract. The dress she selected was similar in style to the one she'd worn the day before: definitely feminine and hinting at sexuality. She tried to subdue the sensuous effect by not unfastening any of the top buttons and by looping a matching scarf around her neck and draping it so no flesh at all was visible. Pat looked at her reflection, then pulled the scarf off, thinking her modesty was ridiculous. Merchand hadn't ravished her, he had simply looked at the opened throat of her dress—and that was the reward the dress had been designed to collect. But without the scarf she couldn't keep her own eyes off the definitely and primly fastened buttons. She put the scarf back on.

Today there were no traffic pileups, and she got to the library a full hour before she was due at Merchand's office. She found the reference section and located some elementary information about the Merchand Corporation: how many shares were in distribution, how many were owned by the founding family, when the last split occurred, the growth percentage, that Merchand Sr. had died two years ago at the age of seventy-seven and control of the company had passed to his son. The blurb was dry and without personal feeling; there was nothing about Derrick Merchand the man.

A librarian helped her locate *Forbes* magazine that contained a feature about Merchand. It was a year old, but the article was two or three pages long and fairly comprehensive. It told how the company had modernized its approach after the younger man had taken over, had leaped in profit and areas of marketing, and had broadened its base. It said they were planning to introduce a line of cosmetics. It said Derrick was a bachelor.

She closed the magazine to recheck the date on the

front, then flipped it open again quickly. His marital status shouldn't interest her; it was of no importance where her job was concerned.

Derrick was a graduate of Yale, thirty-five years old, generous to charity groups, and a recluse of sorts. He occasionally vanished on his sloop for a day or two, but sometimes he was away from contact for weeks at a time. He was scheduled to appear on a nationwide talk show. Then she remembered that the magazine was a year old and he had already made that appearance.

When she was through reading, Pat glanced at her watch and saw twenty minutes remained before her appointment. She didn't want to be early any more than she wanted to be late, and decided to walk if the weather permitted.

Slush, ice, and snow were piled here and there in front of buildings and in alleys, but the temperature had become more mild, the brownish mounds were melting, and no more snow was coming down. This could be the break that presaged spring. She was ready for the season to change—winter had seemed interminable. During most of it, she had been consumed with worry about her mother and the bills, and she had heard about the search for someone to represent the Merchand company in their new campaign. She almost hadn't applied. Many of the modeling jobs were going to very, very young girls, and Patricia was in her twenties—over halfway through them. But Becky's insistence had finally convinced her to try. At the first of the preliminary interviews she found Merchand wanted a representative who was youthful enough to appeal to women in their teens and twenties and thirties, but one with enough maturity and proof of living etched in expression and line of feature so she would also appeal to women in their forties, fifties, and sixties. A round, innocent, cherubic face that had developed no character and was simply pretty to look at wouldn't do. Pat didn't relish the knowledge that she was getting character, but she supposed everyone did if they lived long enough.

Before she got into the elevator to go to the executive offices, she sat on a bench in the lobby and changed from her boots into her shoes. She still had five minutes, so she idled along the upper hall to the reception room, and at exactly one minute until two she opened the door.

"You may go in, Miss Dayton," the receptionist said.

As on the two previous times, she headed for the door to the boardroom.

"Mr. Merchand's office," the woman said.

Patricia glanced at the two doors on the opposite side of the room but couldn't remember which one led to the corridor where his office was. The receptionist pointed. It was two o'clock on the dot. She hurried through the door, along the short hall, and passed through the ornate entrance into the office where Russell sat at his desk. He glanced at her and said nothing, simply gestured toward Merchand's office. Pat sped across the room, opened the door, and stepped inside to see him behind his desk as he had been the day before. But today he didn't have the phone or the pad to distract him.

Merchand glanced at her, then at his watch. "You're only one minute late, Miss Dayton," he said. "An improvement over yesterday."

Patricia couldn't tell him she had stalled and dawdled so she wouldn't be early, and she couldn't say she had got the doors mixed up. She said nothing.

Derrick slipped the button of his coat and shrugged the jacket off. He picked up a contract that lay centered in a cleared space amid the jumble on his desk. "Shall we?"

For a split second Patricia was afraid he had changed his mind and was going to say he had decided on one of the other women. "Yes," she said swiftly.

He got up and strolled to the window. He was as beautifully dressed as he had been the day before and his clothes fit him as well; his trousers showed the line of leg and the swell of tight buttocks. There was something hauntingly familiar about the way he walked.

He turned. "Do you want to read the contract?"

Patricia glanced around uncertainly. She thought other people would be present—witnesses—but maybe they wouldn't come until after she read it, when she signed it. She was certain she would sign. She moved toward Merchand, and as she rounded the group of chairs he sat down on a short and narrow padded bench that was placed parallel to the window. He laid the contract down and looked at her as if daring her to pick it up.

She had no option but to do so. She did—quickly—and stood as she skimmed the first clauses. The contract seemed ordinary enough. It included her duties and what she would be paid: one hundred thousand dollars a year! The sight of the zeros made her knees almost give way.

"Sit down," Merchand said.

He was gazing out the window, ostensibly paying no attention to her, but he had seen her weakness.

The only place for her to sit without walking away from him was on the bench beside him. She hesitated.

He turned from the window and his gaze lifted to lock with hers. "Sit down," he said pleasantly, but with a hint of challenge. His look seemed to ask if she was afraid of him.

She considered going to one of the leather chairs but was sure he would laugh at her if she did. He had nothing personal in mind. She had lived in fantasy so often, she saw suggestions where none existed. She sat, and awareness of him filled more of her concentration than did the printed pages—until she reached the end. Two clauses had been added. She glanced at him.

He met her gaze calmly. "Something wrong?"

"This one." Pat pointed to the clause that said she wouldn't be allowed to marry during the term of her contract.

Merchand leaned toward her and took the page. "Oh, yes," he said matter-of-factly, "the contract is for three years, and we don't want your status to change during that time." He looked at her again and raised an eyebrow. "Do you object? Were you thinking of getting married?"

She shook her head. She hadn't thought of marriage since she and Bart had parted company; she'd wanted no thought of it. But to have to sign an agreement prohibiting it made her wary. That was as binding as a marriage contract, the only difference being that she would know when this contract would end, and one could never be sure of a marriage contract. "I never thought something like this would be in writing," she said.

"We have to protect our interests." He handed the paper back to her. "The publicity you'll get would insure that a wedding would be public knowledge. We want to appeal to a broad spectrum of consumers, and a married woman wouldn't have the same effect on the youth of today. She would be less influencing toward sales to men buying perfume for their ladies.''

"Oh," she said slowly, "I see."

"You agree to it?"

She hesitated only a second longer. "I might as well. I have no intention of marrying."

He smiled. "Never?"

Pat declined to answer. Her personal life was none of his concern. She would have to conduct herself as befitted the Merchand Girl and not marry as long as the contract was in effect, and that was all he needed to know. But as she read the final clause she realized the Merchand Corporation planned to have more to do with her private life than she had ever supposed they would. She was not to be allowed to go anywhere without their okay, and she wouldn't be able to date anyone unless he was approved by the board. By Derrick Merchand, she thought as she glanced at him again. "This last one," she said.

Derrick watched her steadily. "Ah, yes," he said without taking the page. "It occurred to me that would be a justified and political move. We wouldn't want you going just anywhere with just anybody, now, would we? I told you yesterday you might object; that you might feel you were more owned than hired."

"The clause does hint at ownership," she said. "As if I were a bonded servant."

"Right. You wouldn't be a free agent. I told you we have to protect our interests. We have an image to develop and uphold."

"You would have to approve everyone I saw?"

"I'm afraid so. And everywhere you went. You won't be able to, for example, go off on a trip or a vacation unless we approve where you go and for how long." He took the contract from her. "I don't think we're greatly out of line."

"I wouldn't be able to go anywhere without your knowing?"

"No. Nor with anyone of whom we disapproved."

"That seems a little extreme."

"Sometimes, Miss Dayton, extreme measures are the only recourse."

"I knew I'd have to conduct myself according to certain standards, be select about my appearances."

"That's right. That's what this guarantees."

She felt a hot flash of anger at this obvious evidence that he didn't trust her. "I had assumed those agreements would be tacit: that they wouldn't be written down. I knew I'd have to be—be—"

"Watched?"

"Proper. Admirable. An assett."

He nodded. "You will be."

"I would have been even if it wasn't written down," she flared.

"The contract will remain as is, Miss Dayton," Derrick stood and looked down at her. "If you object . . ." He left the unfinished sentence hanging in the air as if it were another challenge he was throwing at her.

She had an impulse to grab the contract from him. She had to have the job even if it meant having to give up her freedom completely. She didn't want to date anyone in particular, so why did she resist? Because sometimes she liked to be alone, she realized. And not to be allowed the privacy to go away where no one could find her was a bit of an imposition. She didn't want to be a fish in a fishbowl, and she would feel like one the moment she signed the contract. For three years she couldn't do anything or go anywhere without Merchand knowing about it.

"Well?" Derrick said. He was looking down at her, waiting for her decision.

She had no real choice. "All right."

He smiled a quick smile, scarcely seen before it was gone, then offered her a hand as she rose. "We'll get witnesses in, then." He went to his intercom.

As Russell and a portly white-haired man came in, Pat sat and looked at the set of contracts, which lay on a hastily cleared edge of Merchand's desk. She breathed deeply once, then scratched her name on each copy, and as she did she felt as if she were signing her life away. She didn't want to be obligated to any man, or be controlled by one; she had been so with Bart. But at least this time she knew where she was going, what she was doing, and when her servitude would end.

Merchand lifted the papers to his side of the desk and signed. "Russell? Harry?" The two men signed and left, and Merchand thrust a copy toward her. "The campaign isn't fully designed, we still have some people to line up, so you'll have a few days off. We'll be in touch." She didn't respond. "Patricia," he said and waited until her gaze raised to his. "And you be in touch if you want to make any plans." He tapped the contract.

"I have no plans."

"Very well." He leaned back and clasped his hands behind his head. "May I ask you something, Miss Dayton?"

"Certainly."

"Where were you last week?"

How did he know she hadn't been in town? Then, with a sinking sensation, she thought maybe they had tried to set up yesterday's session even sooner—and she had been gone! But Becky hadn't heard anything, and no message was on her tape. Maybe they had hung up. "My aunt left me a cottage in Florida," she said. "I was there. I was thinking of selling it."

"Will you?"

She suddenly smiled. "Now I don't have to."

"You like it there." It was a statement, not a question.

"I do. It's lovely. And private."

"Is it?" His eyebrows lifted.

Pat blushed as she thought of her meeting with the fisherman. "Yes, it is, most of the time. It's in a rather remote spot."

"Is it." He was quiet a second. "One other thing, Patricia."

"Yes?"

He leaned forward and put his elbows on the desk. "How did you know where I was yesterday?"

Puzzled, she looked at him. Where else could he have been except at his headquarters to compare the three applicants? "I don't understand."

"During the last half of the session you were looking directly at me."

"I didn't know I was. I couldn't see anything past the lights. I'm sorry."

"Don't apologize. It was that look which tipped the scales in your favor." He leaned back again. "What were you thinking?"

The flush that crept over her this time was unmistakable. "Do I have to tell you what I think as well? Isn't just knowing where I am and who I'm with enough?" Too late, she remembered he was her boss. But he had signed the contract too; he couldn't fire her for being snippy. But that was about the only thing he couldn't fire her for. Nonetheless, she again said, "Sorry."

"Of course you don't have to tell me," he said. "I think that's part of the mystique of your expression. Every man would like to think it's him you're thinking of." He paused a moment. "I guess *I* did. You did look directly at me."

"I was just dreaming."

"Don't forget those dreams, Patricia. They'll bring us a fortune." He sat forward, all business. "And for God's sake don't gain weight. Don't overeat to celebrate your new position. There will be a month's delay before we do any shooting and, as you know, extra weight is justification for us to break the contract."

What could justify her breaking the contract? Everything was in their favor. She had to stay exactly as she was and do exactly as they said, or they could axe her, but she had no option for breaking the contract unless they didn't pay her.

"You may go," Merchand said as if she'd overstayed the bounds of protocol. She got up and headed for the door. She had her hand on the knob when he stopped her. "Miss Dayton." She turned to look at him. "Your aunt's cottage won't be off limits. Any time you wish to go there, just let me know and it'll be approved."

"Thank you. I will." She wanted to bite her tongue for saying thank you, as she shouldn't have to thank him or anyone for permission to go to her own place. She should have said I will and let it go at that.

She started to leave again and once more he said, "Miss Dayton." She turned to him, impatient this time. He was holding a check between his first and second fingers; he fluttered it gently. "Forgetting something?"

Patricia went to the desk, took the check, and left almost at a run.

Though she had the advance, a dazzling twenty-five thousand that came close to making her giddy, her trip home wasn't as joyous and free from worry and tension as the one had been after she'd found out that she had got the job. Now she felt as if she had traded one bondage for another—but one with a time limit: three years. The bondage of debt had seemed endless and with no way out except by selling Rose's cottage.

Signing the contract didn't denote the end of the world, but she was depressed. She would have to tell Merchand everywhere she went, and about everyone she saw. Everyone except the man in her fantasy. She smiled lightly to herself. What could he do about that?

Then a frown replaced her smile as she realized Merchand had the same lean look, the same sensuous quality, as the man in her dreams. She shook her head. No, he didn't. Derrick Merchand was no different from anyone else. Except maybe he was more imperious; he carried himself as if he owned the world and everything in it. She sighed. He did own her. At least for a little while.

When Becky got home and heard about the conditions of the contract, she was more incensed than Pat. "They can't do that to you!"

"I guess they can. I signed the contract."

"But what if you meet someone and want to get married?"

"That's a remote possibility at best, Becky. But if it should happen, if he loves me, he'll wait."

"I don't think I would have signed. Who does that man think he is anyway? God?"

"He might. He runs his company, and he can tell *me* what to do. If you were in my situation, I think you'd have signed as well."

Becky was quiet a minute, then grudgingly agreed. "But now I'll never be able to talk you into going on a double date with Morris and me."

"You didn't have much luck before, Beck. I wasn't interested; I'm still not."

"I bet you'll have to go out with a lot of Dudleys," she said as if she were the one who would have to sit through endless evenings of self-centered conversation.

"Lord, I hope not," Pat said, then grinned. "The contract didn't say I couldn't refuse to go out. And look at the bright side. With the advance, Mom and Dad will be out from under, and if I'm frugal, within two years so will I."

"You'll have to get a new roommate." Becky looked at her in stunned realization. "I hadn't thought of that part of it."

"That part of what?"

"Marrying Morris. When I marry him, I'll move out and you'll have to handle all the rent alone or get another roommate."

"We'll face that when the time comes, Beck. You two haven't even set the date yet."

Derrick tried to go back to work after Patricia left, but he couldn't concentrate. He kept thinking about her. During the entire time he'd been sitting on the bench beside her, he'd had an urge to draw her to him—she had been too far away from him both physically and mentally. But he hadn't, and he felt frustrated. But he could wait. Now that she had signed the contract, he owned her for three years. For that long he would know every step she took.

He wouldn't have given a damn about either of the

other two women; they could have gone where they
wanted with almost anyone they wished. But he wanted
to control Miss Dayton, and he wasn't altogether sure
why. Possibly the wild and uncontrolled way she had
responded to him on the beach had convinced him he
had to control her, and told him she couldn't be
trusted. She herself had admitted she hadn't known
what she was doing.

He wished she had known.

Patricia had no idea it had been he who had her down
in the pine needles on Otter Key; and he hadn't known
who she was at that time either. There had been a mys-
tic quality about that evening—unusual, almost dream-
like. It had bothered him then, and it bothered him
now. He had seen her watching him from the shadows
of the trees the night when he was fishing. He hadn't
expected to see anyone. Since he began construction,
he hadn't seen anyone on the island at dusk. Boaters
and picnickers were always gone on their way so they'd
be in port before nightfall. He thought he had the island to himself.

The second night when he had seen her silhouetted
against the sunset, he knew she was lovely and desirable. Her body was exactly the sort he liked: slender,
slim-waisted, long-legged. And she moved beautifully.
It had been obvious she was looking along the shore for
someone, and he was the only one who'd been there
before for her to see. When he approached her, she
seemed pliable, willing to share the moment. He kissed
her, and she answered with such fire, he was distracted
almost beyond control. But she drew back and became
prim and proper, and had refused him.

He had determined to find out who she was and
when she would return to the island. If he could get

away, he would go as well and love her next time, not be put off—no matter what she said. And after he had returned to his office and was in conference with the board about who to retain to represent the cosmetic line, he had noticed the similarity of Dayton's name to the one who owned the land on the Key. A while back he had offered Dayton a healthy price for the only bit of the island he didn't own and he'd been turned down. But though he wanted the entire place for a retreat, he hadn't worried much about the unowned bit; the locals said the cabin on the south end was seldom used. He should have known someone would visit the empty cottage sometime. When he made the connection between the name of one of his finalists and the person who had refused his offer for her land, then refused him on the beach, he had been angry for both reasons. More important than that, he knew she was indiscriminate and couldn't be trusted to represent Merchand. He had decided against using her, but he had wanted to see her again—in the light this time—and he had. He had seen that look of hers, and he had hired her.

Derrick was amazed by how quickly he changed his mind. He had known from the first that the brunette was too lusty and unreserved to introduce his fledgling line, but he'd been in favor of Miss Land—the blonde. Though she was almost too young, she had strength of expression, and her bones were mature. But when he had seen the three together and seen the way Patricia looked at him, he had known no one would do except her.

He smiled a smile that reached his mind but didn't touch his mouth. Maybe now he wouldn't have to wait to go back to Otter Key to have her. What would she do if she knew it had been he who'd been within a half-second of making love to her that evening? He let his smile touch his lips as he wondered what she'd do the next time.

Damn. Derrick didn't even like models. When he was younger, he had been involved with a few. More than a few. None of them had known anything existed on the other side of the camera except clothes and jewelry, and shops where they could buy those things or have them bought. He hadn't known the female on the beach was a model, or he would never have touched her. But he had.

Derrick had known Pat would sign the contract—she had to. He had done more than check out her name; he knew the debts she had. They were more extravagant than any model's he'd every known—astronomical, at nearly every leading department or jewelry store. Her mother had been ill and financial pressure was on her from that source too. He had felt slightly guilty adding those two clauses to the contract, because he knew she had no choice but to accept them. He had done it anyway. He had always got what he wanted—and he wanted her.

Chapter Six

Two weeks passed and Patricia heard nothing from the Merchand Corporation; the time seemed an eternity. During the day she took long walks, went to her exercise class, window-shopped, and in the evening she stayed home.

A few men she knew phoned and asked her out, but she refused. The idea of having to get permission, tell who she'd be with and where they'd be going, was more than she could face; it made her feel as if she were thirteen and had to ask her parents. She wasn't even sure whom she'd have to tell. Derrick Merchand? The thought made her cringe. Nothing about him let her think of him as a father figure.

Ads Pat had posed for came out in various magazines. One she had done with Jerome was released. She did some of her best work with him, as he did with her. She phoned to compliment him, and he congratulated her on her new job. That was the extent of her social life. She phoned her parents two or three times a week simply to have someone to talk to. She became friends with the delicatessen owner on the corner. Gradually she became discontent with staying home and being lonely—and her loneliness was caused by Derrick Merchand.

Patricia returned to the library and looked him up again. Nothing was listed in the *Readers' Guide* except the *Forbes* article. She got microfilmed issues of newspapers dating from the time he'd taken over the company. In gossip columns she saw his name linked with first one woman, then another. One slightly longer item said he seemed to have given up models and had gone on to professional women.

The slant of the statement made Pat angry. Modeling was a profession, and it was damn difficult work. Maybe modeling didn't require as much formal education as being a lawyer or a doctor or an accountant, but it wasn't a piece of cake either. The article said Derrick had already wooed and won every available and well-known model in the city and had needed new fields to conquer. The reporter was no kinder to him than she was to the modeling profession. Pat smiled as she thought perhaps the writer was envious because he neglected female reporters and columnists; maybe she'd attacked him because of his oversight.

The company finally let her know she hadn't been forgotten: Russell phoned. A conference and a fitting had been scheduled for the next day, and he told her where it would be and when she was expected. The less than three weeks she'd waited had seemed three years long, and she wondered if the actual three years she would represent the company would be as interminable. She would be a hundred years old when it was over, it seemed.

Pat was punctual for her appointment in the fitting room a couple of floors below the executive offices. At least a dozen people were on hand to measure her, fiddle with her hair, drape various types and colors of fabric around her, and revamp her makeup with Merchand products. All this was to give her a special Merchand look. She was handed from one group of reaching arms to another and was kept busy all day.

Late in the afternoon a change affected everyone in the room. Speech was heightened to more clarity of diction, idle chatter stopped, and everyone became more efficient and eager. Derrick had come to see how things were going. Patricia was covered with a white muslin sheet over bra and panties. She was barefoot, her face had been Merchand-ized, and her hair had been washed and trimmed and tugged and fluffed into a cloud around her face. When she saw the cause for the change of atmosphere, she was glad for the sheet; she'd been running around most of the day in nothing but underwear.

Merchand glanced toward her briefly, then became involved in conversation with Florence, the dress designer. His jacket was unfastened and he swept the front of it aside so he could rest his hand on his hip. He had to know the effect his stance had. The long line of his leg showed, the trim swell of his hip, the flat surface of his stomach. He was vain. He knew he was attractive and he advertised it. Pat looked away from him.

A couple of minutes passed before she heard the click of purposeful steps approaching. He was coming toward her, buttoning his coat as he walked.

"Are they treating you all right, Miss Dayton?" he asked.

"Yes, fine."

He stopped in front of her and studied her hair. "I

like that. I knew I would. It gives you the free look I wanted."

So he was the one who had decided how she was to have her hair done. She should have known.

His hand went under her chin, tipped her face upward, and turned it from one side to the other. "Very nice." He seemed unaffected and unconcerned, as if she were no more than a mannequin he'd asked to have decorated. He stepped away from her. "Next week we'll have the official introduction of the Merchand Girl. The word is out that we've hired one and intend to become one of the leaders in the field. We can't wait much longer."

"All right."

"Will you be glad of it? I haven't received any requests from you to go anywhere. You should be happy to get out of the house." He paused. "You haven't gone anywhere, have you? You are keeping to the term of the clause?"

She flashed a look of indignation at him. "Of course I am."

"Good. I've been in Europe for the past couple of weeks, but I left word to be contacted if you began to get cabin fever. I'm glad you were able to stick it out. Better stay under wraps until we officially begin the campaign." As Derrick spoke he touched the sheet as if that were one of the wraps he had in mind. He lifted a corner of it lightly and let it fall. "Very attractive outfit, Miss Dayton. I knew you'd look good in sheets."

The definite sexual overtones weren't missed by Pat. She pulled the cloth more snugly around her, but that only served to outline her curves. "They've been doing fittings."

"I know what they've been doing, Patricia. I told them to do it." He looked at her face again. This time he wasn't looking at a finished product, but at a person. His gaze came to rest on her lips. "Nice," he said. "You'll do very well, I think." He turned and spoke to a number of people as he made his way to the exit.

For a moment Patricia had been sure he was interested in her, and her heartbeat had quickened. She pushed the thought aside. Successful executives had to be concerned with every facet of their businesses. He obviously was, or he wouldn't have brought the company so far along since his father's death. Naturally he would be interested in this branch of the operation, as he'd made the decision to go into the cosmetic field. His father hadn't risked it. Derrick wasn't interested in Patricia Dayton as a person, but as a billboard to advertise his products. And if she could believe what she read, he was after easy conquests, immediate gratification. She didn't like his attitude, his sensual sureness. She wouldn't become a notch in his belt. She didn't care about him. He was her boss and that was all. Their contact was business—only business. She wouldn't let herself be distracted.

Surely they were finished with her. Pat couldn't think of another part of her they could measure or another feature they could enhance. She got off the stool and went behind a screen to dress.

The cosmetologist came to join her before she was half through. Thaddeus wasn't bothered by her semi-nude state; he'd seen women that way too many times to let it bother him. "You have to be here three hours before the grand inauguration," he said. "We'll do your hair and face so you'll be perfect."

"All right."

He touched one of her eyebrows. "Derrick wants this a bit different. A little fuller."

Florence came behind the screen to join them. "Sorry I can't tell you what you'll wear, doll," she said. "Mr. Merchand won't make the decision until the dresses are complete."

"He won't?"

"No. He says he can't visualize them from a sketch, he has to see them finished."

"You mean there's something he admits he can't do?" Patricia asked, and they laughed.

"I doubt it," Thaddeus said. "If it came down to the nitty-gritty, he'd manage with only a sketch."

"Will he have to see me in the clothes?"

Florence shrugged. "He'll let us know."

"I bet he will. And everyone will hop."

Florence looked at her in surprise, and Thaddeus frowned. "Yes, we will," he said. "Because if he asks for something to be done, it's because it's necessary. And we'll do what he says. We're in his employ, after all."

"I know. Sorry." Firmly put in her place, Pat finished dressing. As she started to leave Ryan Murdock, the general coordinator, stopped her.

"You're not to go anywhere between now and your introduction as the Merchand Girl," he said. "Derrick wants you completely out of sight for the week."

"Can I go to the grocery store?" Pat asked tongue in cheek.

"I doubt it." He considered the possibility a moment. "I'll check and let you know."

"Never mind. I'll hide."

And she did. She didn't even go for a walk. When the day came for her to report, she was relieved to be away from her four walls; they had begun to seem like prison bars. She was thirty minutes early, and no one was in the dressing room. She had to wait the half hour before Thaddeus came.

He smiled. "About to go bananas having to stay shut up, huh?"

"You don't know the half of it. Except for my roommate's and the cabdriver's on the way here, yours is the first face I've seen."

"That'll change," he said. "When the campaign is in full swing, you'll be wishing for a bit of privacy." He shoved her head under the tap and began to talk about a Broadway show he'd seen during the past week.

His assistants arrived, and she was plucked, brushed, painted, and dusted until she was sure there wasn't an inch of her they hadn't improved. She was sprayed with a mist of Merchand perfume. Whether the scent would cause men to have a sensuous reaction as it was supposed to do, she didn't know, but she had to admit she smelled better now than she ever had.

Shortly before Pat was scheduled to appear, she was given new underclothes, as if those of her own wouldn't be fine enough to touch the new dress, and then her gown was brought in. It was a soft amber earth tone with touches of muted green and blue as accents. The neckline was crossed folds of fabric that opened and closed fleetingly with her movements, the waist fit snug, and the skirt was full and swept at her knee. Her hose shimmered a slightly darker shade than the dress and were of the finest weave she'd ever worn. The shoes were simple pumps the color of her hair.

When she looked in the mirror, she could scarcely believe what she saw. She had looked pretty before—even beautiful—but this was incredible. An ethereal quality hovered around her, making her seem an unreal vision.

"Did Mr. Merchand choose this?" she asked, fingering the dress.

Florence nodded. "He didn't have to see you model the clothes after all, did he, doll? The moment he saw it, he knew exactly which dress he wanted. It was originally in cream and pink and blue, but we had to do it up in those colors."

"You did?"

"Yes. Derrick said he wanted earthy tones because they'd suit you better. They do."

Patricia had to admit he had excellent taste. The dress wouldn't have done nearly as much for her in any other colors. "It's lovely," she said and smiled at Florence. "*I'm* lovely."

"That you are. Derrick wouldn't have settled for less."

Pat couldn't get enough of her reflection. She had been transformed, and she loved it. The new hairdo and the extra fullness in her brows were the touches that changed hers from just a pretty face into a memorable one. How had Merchand known? She spun and turned in front of the floor-length mirror, trying to see every side of herself.

A few minutes before she had to make her appearance, Derrick came into the room. She lost interest in herself the moment he entered. He looked as exquisite as she did, and he hadn't had a staff working over him for the past hours. At least as far as she knew he hadn't.

He was freshly shaved and his hair was perfectly groomed—maybe he'd had a barber. He was in a blue tuxedo that fit him delightfully. The pants were almost indecently snug, his ruffled shirt was the same pale color as her dress, and his cummerbund picked up the green accents of her gown. They were a matched pair.

He came to her and told her to turn around. She did, then looked at him for approval.

"You'll do," he said.

Do? She was magnificent. She was fantastic. "Thanks a lot."

A contented smile touched his mouth. "We'll let others supply ordinary compliments. I'm a perfectionist, and if I say you'll do, you will." Derrick held out his arm for her. "Shall we?"

For a moment she hesitated. But she'd be expected to be with him, as she was his creation and the cosmetic line was his baby. She looped her arm under his and looked up at him impishly. "You'll do too."

"I certainly hope so." He was solemn. "But it is what's underneath that counts. These clothes are just the shells we wear to console other people." He let his gaze travel over her from head to toe. "If you weren't good beneath, there would be little we could do to make it right."

Pat didn't know whether he was talking about her body or her soul. And she didn't ask.

He led her to the elevator, down, and into a gigantic reception room. The moment they entered a subdued murmur of approval swept the crowd and flashbulbs began to go off. "See?" he said. "Now you'll get compliments."

And she did: from men and women, old and young.

She was photographed from every angle and admired from every eye. Merchand stayed near her. During the entire session he was never more than a few steps away, and more than once she saw a look of admiration in his eyes. He was the center of almost as much attention as she, and when he had to answer questions about his company and the new endeavor, he did it with casual friendliness and unabashed confidence in himself.

All Patricia had to say was that she was pleased to be working with the Merchand Corporation and was delighted with the company's cosmetic products. She was asked a few personal questions: where had she come from, how had she begun her career, what she did for a social life. She answered without worry. She didn't mention Bart.

Jerome was there and congratulated her. He told her he was trying to be selected as one of the photographers who would do some of the stills of her.

"He likes my work," Jerome said. "He's seen some ads we did together and was favorably impressed."

She didn't have to ask who *he* was. She knew: Merchand. "I'm glad, Jerome. I hope you get the job. I enjoy working with you."

"You make it easy," he said.

Merchand took her arm and led her away from him. "Mix," he said softly to her.

She'd been mixing; she'd spent no more time with Jerome than with anyone else. Wasn't she going to be allowed to prefer one person above anyone else?

As the session wore on, Pat realized she wasn't. She could have been talking to Mr. Something-or-Other for less than a minute, and Merchand's hand fastened on her arm and guided her away. The afternoon was nearly over before she realized he left her alone when she spoke with women. The next time he took her away from someone she faced him with it. "You let me talk to women for minutes on end, but you don't let me talk to men. Why?"

Derrick looked disbelieving. "Do I?"

"Yes, you do."

"Well." He was quiet a moment. "There's a totally different aspect involved when you talk to men. We don't want you linked with any particular male. You're going to have to be tremendously careful about that."

A touch of rebellion rose in her. He could go out with whomever he pleased, go anywhere he wished, and she wasn't sure she'd have a date or even an outing for three years.

"Yes. I *did* sign that contract, didn't I?"

"You did."

The final two clauses, the belatedly added ones, flew to her mind. The last one bothered her most. He should have known she'd be particular and discreet, but he'd had the restrictions put in writing. She didn't like to be mistrusted; she was trustworthy. She wouldn't bring disgrace to his company.

Pat glanced at her gown and at the gathering of people and knew Derrick had a great deal at stake. That was why he was constrictive. And she would benefit tremendously from having been chosen as the Merchand Girl. Her resentment was a little out of line. "I'll live up to it," she said.

"Yes. You will." Derrick smiled as he spoke, and she wasn't sure whether he'd been laying down the law or if he had faith in her loyalty.

Champagne was poured and toasts were given for his

success in the new venture and to her success as his emissary. She and Derrick were the first to leave. "We'll let them hash it over now," he said.

In the elevator he reached for her bodice and took a fold of cloth between his thumb and fingers. His touch on her skin inside the cloth was like an electric shock. She hadn't expected the contact and stepped away from him.

He looked at her innocently. "It's a bit out of place." His hand went again to the fold. He moved it a fraction of an inch, looked at it, adjusted it once more infinitesimally, then nodded as if now she were fit to be seen. His hand took an incredible length of time to draw from beneath her dress.

"What are you doing?" Pat asked breathlessly. But she knew what he was doing; he was making her vitally aware of him.

"Fixing your dress."

"Am I all right now?" Her voice was unstable.

"Yes. You're fine."

When the elevator doors slid open, she started down the hall. "Miss Dayton."

"Yes?" She turned to look at him. He was holding the elevator door open. He was so delightful in his tuxedo, so sophisticated, so beautiful—so masculine. He was the most compelling man she'd ever met.

"I would take you to dinner," he said, "but I have a conference about the advertising campaign."

"That's okay," she said, and flushed because it wasn't okay; she'd love to go out with him. She couldn't think of any man she'd rather be with.

He shifted to put his back against the rubber insert of the door, and as it tried to close but caught the presence of his mass and slid into its slot again, he moved gently.

One of his feet was in the elevator, the other outside in the corridor with her. "Be careful who you're seen with," he said, surging lightly as the door tried again to close.

"I will."

"Don't forget to ask." He let his gaze sweep over her. "It's official now. You're Merchand's girl." He drew his leg inside the elevator. "We'll be in touch."

Patricia stared at the door as it finally shut. The Merchand Girl, not Merchand's girl, she thought. Nothing about the man was the least bit insecure, nothing was the least bit resistible. He was gorgeous and cocksure of himself. Now she knew how he could have gone through half the women in New York without a murmur to slow him down. He had such allure about him, he'd have no difficulty seducing anyone he pleased. He probably didn't even need to try, women were probably always trying to seduce him. But she wouldn't. She didn't want to get involved with him like so many other models had. Being his employee was quite enough.

With a swirl of skirts she turned and went to the dressing room. She changed into her own clothes and left before anyone else came in.

The next morning Pat's picture was in every paper: sometimes she was alone, sometimes she was with Derrick. She studied the pictures of him more than those of herself—she'd seen pictures of herself before. The cut of his tuxedo did nothing but enhance his physique. He was a devilishly handsome, rugged man.

He's your boss! she reminded herself for the thousandth time; she shouldn't think of him as anything other than her employer.

But try as she might, she couldn't keep her mind off

how he had looked and how he had looked at her and
how the lines of electricity had followed the slow
course of his hand when he had removed it from her
bodice. Her dress hadn't needed to be straightened.
They had left the reception; no one save he was to see
her in the dress again that day.

Chapter Seven

The next week William James, a friend of Pat's family, came to town and wanted to take her to dinner and a show. Obediently, though reluctantly, she phoned the Merchand offices, got the executive receptionist, Mrs. Kelsoe, and told her who the man was and where they planned to go. The woman asked her to hold and she'd put Merchand on the line.

Patricia hung up.

If she had to ask Derrick personally, she wouldn't go anywhere. Her friend could come to the apartment for dinner, and Becky could invite Morris. They'd have a pleasant and private evening at home. The more she thought about having to tell Merchand everything she did, the more she resented that clause of the contract. Where was Derrick going this evening? He didn't have to tell anyone, didn't have to ask; he could freely go out on the town with a beautiful lawyer or doctor or architect. Or he could work. She had heard he often worked twelve to sixteen hours a day, either at corporation headquarters or at one of the subsidiary companies. She hoped he had to work.

She phoned Becky to ask if she'd agree to the new plan, then called William to tell him of the change.

Now she was faced with the prospect of cooking dinner, and there was nothing on hand fit for guests. She wasn't a gourmet cook by any stretch of the imagination, but she could make a decent lasagna. She bundled up to go to the store for the ingredients, salad fixings, and a bottle of red wine. She hadn't been home ten minutes before the phone rang.

"You have a date for tonight," Merchand said. "Wear something elegant."

She felt an instant sense of antagonism at his imperious command. "Mr. Merchand—" She stopped. How could she refuse to go? If Russell or the receptionist or any underling had called, she would have said she couldn't make it because she had company coming.

"I phoned earlier, but you were out." He put a strange inflection on the word out. "Where were you?"

"I was shopping," she said. "Do I have to get permission to buy groceries?"

He ignored her snippy question, said "Your date will pick you up at seven thirty," and hung up.

Pat looked at the phone as if it had betrayed her. She hated the blasted things anyway, they only transferred words, there was never an expression to read, no way to exchange real information. Just words. She slammed the receiver onto its hook. Wear something elegant, indeed. What if she didn't want to go? What if she didn't own anything elegant? She did, though. Bart had seen to that.

For a few minutes she slumped petulantly on the couch and thought maybe if she put on jeans, whoever her date was wouldn't wait around. She didn't even know who she had a date with; just that he'd be calling for her at seven thirty.

Her stubborn mood didn't last. She *had* signed the contract. She'd been on PR dates for the agency, and she should have expected Merchand would do the same sort of thing—select her dates, not only have to approve a person she chose. She hoped her escort wouldn't be too much of a loser.

Once again she called Becky and William, this time to tell them dinner was off because she had an appointment.

By seven thirty she was ready, dressed in a black gown that was the only fashionable one she owned. It was a simple gown and had cost a fortune. So had the simple pendant and earrings. And none of them was paid for yet.

At seven thirty-five Pat began to wonder if she'd misunderstood the time. By seven forty she was impatient and tempted to take off the dress and forget it. If she had to be punctual, why couldn't her date be? This had to be part of his job too. At seven forty-one the doorbell rang.

She took her time answering; she was still irritated that Derrick had ordered her to go out. But when she opened the door and saw her boss, her pulse rate increased immediately, and that irritated her more.

Derrick was quiet, just looking at her, obviously waiting for her to say something, and she realized she hadn't greeted him. "Hello," she said finally.

"Am I late?"

"Of course not."

"Yes, I am. I'm exactly eleven minutes late."

She had been ten minutes late for the meeting with the board, one minute late when she went to sign the contract. "I wasn't late for those meetings deliberately," she said defensively.

A smile flicked his mouth. "I wasn't deliberately late either, but as I was hurrying along the corridor I looked at my watch and saw I was late by eleven minutes. I think that's amusing. Now we're even."

Pat wondered if she'd ever be even with him, and knew she wouldn't: he was the boss, he could tell her what to do. She glanced past him. "Where's my date?"

He spread his hands. "You're looking at him."

"You?"

Derrick smiled. "Can you think of anyone the Merchand Corporation would approve more quickly?"

She backed up a step. "But—You!"

"Is there something wrong with me?" He glanced at himself as if to spot what it was, could find nothing wrong, and looked at her again. "I had a free evening, and if you're living up to the terms of the contract by letting us know where you go and with whom, you haven't stuck your nose out of your apartment since you signed with us. So we're going out."

"But I—" Pat started to tell him he should know that she'd phoned for permission, then stopped. Maybe the receptionist hadn't told him she'd called.

"There couldn't be a better way to highlight the campaign than for the Merchand Girl to be seen with the president of Merchand," he said with undeniable logic. "Therefore, if you have no objection...." He gestured along the hall to indicate she should precede him.

"I have to get my coat." She went to fetch it from the couch. It was the only coat she owned, as she had let the furs Bart had selected go back. As she returned to the door she put it on.

Derrick looked at her critically, and as they went toward the elevator he said, "We'll let you borrow a wrap."

"Thank you, no. I'd rather wear my own."

"Then I'll buy you a coat."

"No, you won't." Her eyes sparked with defiance. He might be her boss for three years, but he wasn't going to go any farther than the terms of the contract. He wasn't going to buy her a coat as if he were keeping her.

He jabbed a finger at the call button. "Miss Dayton, you work for me and your image reflects on Merchand. You'll do as I say."

"There was nothing in the contract that said you could buy me a coat," she flared. "Only that you approve where I go and who I go with." She lifted her eyebrows. "And that's why I'm with you."

The elevator doors hissed open; three people were inside. They rode downward to the accompaniment of mechanical clunks and rattles; no one spoke. Patricia didn't look at Merchand, but she could feel his gaze on her. He was probably thinking she looked like something the cat dragged in. She lifted her chin a little higher; this was her coat and it was paid for.

He didn't talk as he guided her to his waiting car, started the powerful engine, and darted from the curb without looking to see if anyone was coming. She glanced at him. His jaw was set, as if he had been crossed, she thought. He was spoiled, he'd always got what he wanted before, and because she wouldn't wear a borrowed wrap or let him buy her one, he was irritated. She wondered why, if he was so angry, he didn't simply march her back to her door and leave.

After what seemed a year of silence, Pat could take it no longer. "Where are we going?"

"Dining and dancing," he said shortly.

He seemed so out of temper at the prospect, his

emotion flooded over onto her. "You don't have to do it, you know. I was perfectly content to stay home."

"I know I don't have to do it. But we can't generate much interest in the Merchand Girl if she stays cooped in her flat all the time, now, can we?"

She shut up and stayed quiet. This outing was part of the campaign; it was part of his work and part of hers.

Derrick halted the car so abruptly, she dipped forward and had to brace her hand on the dashboard. She looked accusingly at him, but he was already getting out of the car. The doorman opened her door, and Merchand came to take her arm in a firm grasp. "Smile," he said. "Reporters and columnists will be here, and we don't want them to think you're unhappy about our company, do we?"

He herded her inside and, as soon as they were out of the cold, helped her off with her coat and quickly handed it to the hatcheck girl. When they were within sight of other people, his entire attitude changed: his arm went familiarly around her waist and his head tipped toward her. "Smile," he repeated, more softly this time.

Pat glanced at him and saw his expression was one of satisfaction: he seemed pleased with her and the entire situation. If he could pretend, so could she. Too she supposed she could lose her job if she didn't do as he told her. She smiled.

Derrick introduced her to a number of people, and she greeted them serenely, trying to exude pride at being the Merchand Girl. She should be proud. And she would have been if her boss didn't behave in such a cavalier manner—the lord of everything he surveyed. Pat wished he had sent her with a Dudley, even though being with Derrick was the most political move his corporation could make and their appearance together would accentuate the new line. Tomorrow her name would be linked with his—another model for Merchand—but this one would be called the Merchand Girl, and people would think of Merchand cosmetics.

They went to a booth, and the waiter moved the table aside so they could sit. Merchand sat near her and draped an arm behind her in a possessive manner. They weren't in the best location, though they were relatively visible. If he had planned ahead, surely they would have been dead center. He obviously hadn't decided on the date until he learned she already had plans. He had scheduled this dinner to keep her from seeing her friend. Mrs. Kelsoe *had* told him.

More than a dozen people came over to exchange words with him, and he was gracious and introduced Patricia. On occasion he bent to tell her who was coming and how she should behave. His breath stirred her hair as he spoke, and the warmth from his arm where it lay casually behind her radiated onto her skin, but she didn't want to be aware of the intimate feel of him. He had deliberately intervened in her plans. The only reason the man was with her tonight was because she'd had something else to do. The more she thought about why she was here, the madder she got.

When the waiter came for their orders, she said she didn't want to eat. Merchand ordered for her.

Over the back of their booth she could see the dance floor below their level. Beyond was a small platform that held a three-piece band playing gentle, melodic pieces: dentist-office music that didn't interfere with conversation. The consideration made no difference to her, for she and Merchand had nothing to say to each other.

After they were served, she couldn't eat. Merchand said, "When I told you not to gain weight, I didn't mean you should starve yourself."

"I'm not hungry."

"Eat." He cocked an eyebrow at her. "If you lose weight, I'll fire you for that too."

Patricia glared at him and had an almost irresistible urge to tell him he could shove his job. She couldn't do that, though; she'd already sent the advance to her parents. Unwillingly she picked up her knife and fork and began to play with her food.

"That's better," he said.

Again she glanced at him. Why had he hired her? she wondered. He didn't seem to like anything she did. Perhaps one of the interviews should have been a date with the boss, then he could have learned how each of the applicants behaved. And they could have discovered how imperious he was.

Pat managed to get down a few bites as Derrick finished his meal. After he pushed his plate aside, he pulled out a slim cigar. "Do you mind if I smoke?"

"No. Go on."

Derrick lit the cigar and as he smoked he watched her toy with her food. "Do I make you lose your appetite?"

He was part of the reason she couldn't eat, but not all of it. The idea of being on show, of having to mind him, of being restrained, served to dampen her appetite. "No," she said. "I'm sorry. It's just that this is new to me."

"You've never eaten in a restaurant before?"

Her tongue clicked at the ridiculous question. "You know what I mean."

"Do I?"

Irritation flared in her again. Why did he have to be so obtuse? "Of course you do." She made a gesture to indicate the other people. "This."

"Being on display?"

"Yes. And being told everything to do."

He smiled—the most minimal smile she'd ever seen. "I'll tell you something else to do. Look pleasant. An expression like the one you have now will lead everyone to think we're having a quarrel. I'm sure they would imagine you'd be happier with Merchand than that."

Her eyebrows shot up. "The man or the product?"

Derrick glared at her. "Both. But if not with the man, certainly with the product. You look as though you're being forced against your will."

"And I'm not?"

"No, you're not."

"You can tell me where to go, who to go with, what to do. I have no say about my life anymore."

"*This* is terrible?" He made the expansive gesture she had made a moment before.

It wasn't, but how she had got there wasn't absolutely the best. "Not really."

"Look, Patricia, I warned you you might feel owned, and you signed the contract anyway, so, dammit, look for one minute as if you're enjoying yourself."

"All right," she whispered. Actually, she could blame no one but herself. She closed her eyes for a second, then looked at him and generated a glorious smile. "Is this better?"

Impulsively he touched her cheek, then jerked his hand away. "Yes. Better." His jaw clenched and the muscle jumped a few times. He looked at the ash on his cigar and rolled it into the ashtray.

Now he was looking like he didn't want to be there, Pat thought, as if clouds had formed in his mind and a thunderstorm might break at any minute. He was hunched over, playing with the tip of his cigar in the ashes—flattening them, spreading them neatly and evenly along the bottom of the dish. He was attractive, with dark brows perfectly shaped to fit his forehead, straight nose, and a clean-shaven, strong jaw—which was still clenched—and finely shaped lips that Pat longed to kiss. Under any other circumstances she'd love to be seen with him.

Derrick looked up and caught her studying him. He watched her eyes a moment, then asked, "Shall we dance?"

The words caused a vision of an old movie to pop into her head. She grinned. "Are you Fred Astaire?"

He frowned. "No. But I won't embarrass you." He stubbed out his cigar, slid out of the booth, and pulled her to her feet. He'd never touched her so gently before, but he was still frowning.

Derrick was thinking the woman was impossible. When he was in fairly good spirits and wanted to make the evening a success, she was recalcitrant, and when he'd almost given up and written the outing off as a dead loss, she turned on the charm. He wasn't sorry he had selected Patricia to represent his company because she photographed beautifully and that look of hers was inimitable, but the fact that he'd chosen to be interested in her personally bothered him. He could have sent someone else with her this evening, since he wanted to keep her from going out with someone she had chosen. But he hadn't.

He led her to the dance floor as if she were just anyone, then he took her in his arms and knew she wasn't:

she was the dryad from the beach and she fit against him perfectly. He shoved her away and she glanced at him quizzically. "Do you know what you're doing?" he asked.

"Of course I do."

Derrick watched her for a moment, thinking about how she'd behaved on the Key, how, to get out of making love with him, she'd said she didn't know what she was doing. He sighed and drew her to him again. "I'm not sure I do."

Patricia hovered on the brink of dropping into fantasy: many things about Derrick reminded her of the man in her dreams, or was that the fisherman? She'd never been so emotionally stirred by a man. The electricity that had followed his hand that time in the elevator hadn't been imagined, for now the touch of him along her length made her entire body aware.

As he'd promised, he didn't embarrass her: he was one of the finest dancers she'd ever been on a floor with, but Pat came close to doing something that would have embarrassed them both—herself anyway. She wanted to wrap her arms around his neck and kiss him. The idea was so compelling, she gripped the fabric on his shoulder to make her hand stay where it was.

Her partner felt the convulsive movement and looked at her. His eyebrow lifted as if he knew why she was clutching so tightly to his shoulder, then he held her to him as in an embrace and his mouth nuzzled her hair. And she didn't resist him; he felt so good and so wonderful, she wanted to melt into him.

"You have a desirable body," Derrick murmured.

It seemed to take a full minute for the words to make the passage through the complicated channels of her ear and join with the complex circuits of her brain so they would register, and at the same time they did, she realized she was so close to him, they were touching from knee to shoulder. And their closeness wasn't all because of the firm, ardent grasp he had on her: she was pressing eagerly and happily into him, relishing the strong, masculine feel of his body.

Abruptly she pulled from him. "I think we'd better sit down."

"So do I." His voice was rough with obvious desire and his eyes were clouded.

For a moment she thought he was going to kiss her, and she leaned toward him—drawn by a magnet—but he didn't, he just led her to the table. After they sat, Pat glanced at him warily. She'd offered herself so wantonly, he couldn't have missed it, and now she didn't know what to do or say. She scarcely knew Derrick— she hadn't seen him but a few times, two of those only briefly—and he was her boss. But she'd held him so fondly, had been so ready to kiss him. She began to search through her clutch bag as if she were looking for something. And she was: self-composure.

Derrick leaned forward and brushed the backs of his fingers across her cheek. When she looked at him, they moved to lightly caress the fluff of her hair, moving it gently. His gaze fastened on her lips and, again, she was sure he was going to kiss her. He moved his hand to the side of her neck and let it drift across her shoulder; his touch was vital to her as it slid slowly down her arm. Her gaze dropped to his lips and his tongue came out to dampen them. She couldn't stop hers from doing the same.

"Want some dessert?" he asked so softly, she almost didn't catch the words.

"No, thank you."

"I do," he said, low and ardent. "You."

Her head moved jerkily from side to side in a mannequin's imitation of no. She wanted him; she wanted him badly, but all she would be to him was dessert—no more and no less—a sweet confection to top off the meal, round out the evening. She knew what he thought of models; she knew his reputation with them.

"You want me," he murmured.

"Mr. Merchand, I only work for you," Pat said, striving to make her voice seem cool and normal, "and I don't do that sort of thing, so put it out of your mind. Besides, I scarcely know you."

"You know me better than you think," he said and leaned back in his chair. He wondered if now was the time to tell her he had been the man on Otter Key, that she had kissed him with complete abandon, that he had touched her and he wanted oh so badly to touch her again. He decided against it. A better time would come; for now he would keep that episode separate from their lives. "Want some coffee?" he asked.

"No, thank you."

"I think I will." He gestured for the waiter and ordered.

He took his time, lit another cigar, and let his gaze wander idly over the room. They were as silent as they had been during the earlier part of the evening. Once he glanced at her. "Are you sure?"

She wasn't certain what he was talking about, but she was positive yes would be the correct answer and uttered the single syllable.

"It's very good coffee," he said as if that were the only invitation he'd had in mind.

When his cup was empty, he looked at her once more. "Would you like to dance again?"

Pat almost said yes, but was afraid to be that near to him. She shook her head.

"I wish you would. We dance well together."

"I—" She cleared her throat. "I think not.

He frowned, knowing her refusal was because of a fear of him. He had asked, she had said no, he wasn't going to push the issue. Perhaps he should have waited until they knew each other better. Derrick stood and dropped a tip onto the table. "If we aren't going to dance again, we may as well leave." He sounded petulant, and he didn't like that, but dammit, he wanted to hold her again. She'd been so warm and free on the island and here she was as prickly as a rosebush.

After he retrieved her coat, he helped her into it. "You really do need a new coat, love," he said. "I think we can work one into the perks awarded you; that way receiving one won't offend your sense of right and wrong." He was doing it again—snipping at her, but he couldn't stop. "You do have an image to project. Merchand's. Mine. Either way you phrase it, it's the same."

Patricia knew he was right, so she didn't argue: her coat was a loser and dreadfully out of style. However, she wore it with dignity as they waited for his car to be brought around.

At her apartment building he pulled into an empty parking space. "You needn't come up," she said. "I can make it on my own."

"Foolish girl," he said. He was out and on the sidewalk before she'd opened her door. His hand was gentle, the merest touch on her elbow.

"Just to the building door," she said.

"Your door."

She stopped. "That isn't necessary."

Derrick put his hands on his hips. "What's wrong? Do you think I'll attack you in the hallway?"

"No, I—"

"Are you afraid you won't be able to resist inviting me in?"

She flushed. "Of course not."

He shrugged grandly. "Well, then, what's the problem?"

He was so logical, he'd make her smile if she wasn't so fearful of her response to him. "None, I guess."

"Very well." Derrick took her arm, in a more definite way this time, and led her inside.

Silently they rode up together and, after they got out of the elevator, he took her arm again and ushered her to her door. "Safe so far."

"Thank you," Pat said, glancing at him, "for dinner."

"I don't think you need to thank me. You ate very little."

"I didn't feel much like eating."

"That's right. You had your mind on other"—he paused a fraction of a second—"things."

She was instantly warm with embarrassment. "I did not."

"Oh? Weren't you thinking about the campaign?" He looked ultimately innocent.

She wasn't going to pursue this conversation. "Good night."

"Patricia," he said, suddenly afraid she'd open her door and vanish inside. "I'd like to kiss you." His gaze played over her face and came to rest on her lips.

"I'm not your dessert," she said.

He shook his head slowly. "No. I think you'd make

an entire meal. Kiss me.'' He was only a half-foot away and it was an easy matter for him to pull her against him. His gaze lingered on her lips, then his mouth brushed hers swiftly and tantalizingly. He looked into her eyes again. ''Now, that wasn't so bad, was it?''

It hadn't been bad at all; his touch had been filled with voltage. She could feel the lure of him coursing through her; she hadn't felt so alive since that man had kissed her on Otter Key. She felt exactly the same way: heady and without reserve. He kissed her again and his tongue touched her closed lips. The contact sent another charge through her, and she grew weak with want. She had to resist him; she couldn't give in to his appeal. He thought because she worked for him, because she was a model, he had the right to take liberties. ''Don't—don't do that. You don't own me, Mr. Merchand, even if you think you do. Maybe the corporation does in a way, but not you.''

''I don't? But I want to, Patricia. I want you.''

She backed up a step, afraid if she didn't get away from him now she never would. She wanted him more than any man she'd ever seen; she had wanted him since the first moment she had seen him. She backed up another step and bumped into the wall.

Derrick put one hand on either side of her, his palms flat against the wall, and his head lowered to her. His tongue traced her top lip, then his lips met hers in a perfect kiss, but he let it last only a moment, then he drew away. ''I wouldn't object if you changed your mind and invited me in.''

''I wouldn't dream of it,'' she said, already doing that.

''Oh, you can dream of it if you wish, but you'd better not do it, because I'd accept.'' He touched her lips with his again, lightly. "Good night, Patricia," he said softly, pushed abruptly back, and went toward the elevator.

She resisted a strong desire to call to him and stop him. As the elevator doors opened and he stepped inside, he glanced at her. And only after he was gone did she gain the strength to move.

Chapter Eight

The next Monday Russell phoned and told Patricia to report to Ryan Murdock, the coordinator of the campaign, for a work schedule; she was to meet him on the floor where she'd been fitted. That was a couple of floors beneath Derrick's office, but she could have a chance meeting with him. She didn't know what she'd do or how she'd behave the next time she saw him.

Cautiously, alert for the sight of him, she went into the building. She reached the dressing room without seeing him, and that both relieved and disappointed her. Ryan was waiting for her and he presented her with a demanding schedule: they were to do an extensive series of stills to be used for newspapers, magazines, and billboards; later they would do action shots for television.

She had to report in the mornings, sometimes ridiculously early, to be worked over by Thaddeus and his crew. She was shampooed and groomed and made up to perfection, then she went to the studio or to the location for the day. There, she posed in one or more outfits with one or more Merchand products. Sometimes she was photographed alone and sometimes there was a background with one or more persons. When she was

alone, the shooting went more smoothly with fewer de-
lays, and when they worked in the studio, the effi-
ciency was better because they had control over the
environment.

Again, she fell into the habit of dropping into fantasy. The man in her dreams had picked up a lot of
Derrick's characteristics, he even said things to her
Merchand had said. At first she tried to keep her fantasies from happening. Failing that, she tried to prevent
the gradual takeover of her fantasy man by Merchand.
She had to surrender on each effort because it was
easier to work when she was in dream, and she pleased
the photographers more—especially Jerome, who had
landed one of the contracts.

Pat didn't see her boss, but she knew he was seeing
the pictures of her and, though she received no feed-
back on what he thought, she knew he approved. If he
hadn't, he'd have let her know.

She always had Sunday off—and Saturdays, if they
had met the schedule for the past week—but she didn't
go anywhere. She didn't have the inclination.

One free Saturday, Russell called in midafternoon
and told her she had a date for the evening. She wasn't
told with whom or where she'd be going, simply when
and to be elegant. And she was sure she'd see Derrick.
Nearly a month had passed since she'd seen him, but
her dreams had made him closer and more intimate
than if she had. She was afraid to go with him; she
couldn't risk it. She wouldn't go.

When at eight the doorbell rang, Pat was dressed in
jeans and her hair was tucked under a turban, because
she knew Merchand wouldn't take her out looking like
this. But she was afraid to answer the door, afraid what
his reaction to her defiance would be. She got a bit of

false bravado together, and by the time she reached the door, her courage had grown. She threw it back with a flourish. He wasn't there; Shelby Arthur was, the oldest member on the board of directors.

Shelby looked at her in amazement, which rapidly turned to chagrin. "They must not have advised you of our appointment for this evening," he said.

"I—" She stopped, deciding to take the coward's way out. "What appointment?"

"There's a meeting of fashion designers at Lincoln Center. Derrick thought it might be advisable to be there to show you off."

"I didn't know." In a way it was the truth, for she hadn't known what she was expected to attend. "I can be ready in an hour."

"I'm afraid by then the conference will have ended."

"Half an hour?" she offered.

"I don't know. We were to make only a brief appearance. They began at six, and we don't want to arrive when they're leaving. That wouldn't be politic at all. No, not at all."

"I'm sorry," Pat said, and she was. The poor man looked distressed by the situation.

"I can't understand how you couldn't have been told. Things are usually better organized than this." He smiled kindly at her. "Well, it can't be helped this time, I don't suppose. But I'll send out a memorandum to the effect that there's a snarl in our communications with you."

Patricia grabbed his arm. She wanted to stop him from sending a memo, tell him she'd been informed, but she didn't. "I'm sorry," she repeated.

"Can't be helped, I don't suppose. Can't be helped." With another kindly look at her, he left.

She shut the door and leaned against it. Now she was in for it. She was supposed to be available to represent the company; she could be fired for doing what she'd done.

"Beck," she called out to her roommate, "I'm going to be killed."

"Who's going to kill you?" Becky asked, striding into the living room.

"My boss."

"Whatever for? You said you didn't have to agree to go out, just that they have to approve any plans you make."

"This was different. I have to make appearances when they're requested. That has nothing to do with the final clause."

"Then why'd you refuse?"

"I thought Mr. Merchand was to take me. I didn't want to go with him."

"Why not?"

She didn't want to talk about her ambivalent feelings toward Derrick. He lured her and excited her, but she didn't want to submit to his dominance, his sexual sureness. She didn't want to be just another conquest for him. "He's overbearing," she said. "He's, he's... bossy."

Becky grinned.

"Don't say it! I swear I'll hit you if you do. I know he's my boss and has the right to be bossy, but he never finds anything about me to approve. He never gives positive reinforcement. He thinks he knows everything. He's critical." She paused and looked at Becky with a sense of doom. "And now he has something to criticize."

During the weekend she could scarcely sleep, and when she arrived for work on Monday, she was told to report to Merchand's office immediately.

"At seven o'clock in the morning?" she said unbelievingly to Thaddeus.

He looked surprised at her remark. "Derrick is usually at work by this time. Did you think we were the only early birds around here? Go on. We'll wait for you to get back."

"I can't go dressed like this," she protested. When she was due for a sitting, she didn't put on makeup or do anything with her hair. She was bare-faced and had a scarf wrapped around her head. She wore duck trousers and a baggy sweat shirt. Merchand would fire her if he knew she wandered the streets of New York looking like this.

"I guess you have to," Thaddeus said. "He said immediately upon your arrival. And when he says immediately, he doesn't mean in ten minutes or even five—he means now."

"Oh, Lord," she said.

"Things will only be worse if you keep him waiting; he knows when you arrive each day. Someone has probably already reported your appearance."

"Oh, Lord," Pat said again. She thought of chucking the job without the formality of being told never to darken the doors of Merchand again.

"As scared as you look, I'd guess you did something to offend our boss," Thaddeus said.

"I did," she admitted in a small voice.

"He won't skin you alive," he said with a light chuckle. "He'll only flay you with words."

Surely Merchand would understand why she'd done what she'd done. The only other time she had been ordered to get ready for a date had been to go with him. Okay. If he wanted to fire her, let him.

She marched out of the fitting room, down the hall, to the elevator. Her confidence stalled as she went into the reception room. No one was there. She went across the room, into the short corridor, and to the ornate doorway and office. Russell wasn't there. She was beginning to feel no one in the world existed except her and the man she had to face. Walking on eggshells, she crossed the room, but stopped at his door, dreading to go in.

Pat opened the door to see Merchand behind his desk. He stopped writing and looked at her. The movement of the pen through the light grip of his fingers and his expression of utter disapproval sanctioned Patricia's initial dread. Derrick said nothing but continued to stare at her and toy with the pen. Pat felt smaller than the object he held. She had done wrong.

Derrick dropped his gaze and laid the pen deliberately and precisely in the middle of the pad in front of him. He took an unconscionable length of time getting it lined up in the exact center, then his eyelids flew up and he was looking at her again.

Pat wanted to fall through the floor. He was dreadfully angry with her. "Mr. Merchand," she said, but the sound couldn't have traveled the short distance across the room.

"Sit down, Miss Dayton," he said and watched as she unglued herself from the doorway and crossed toward him.

She was glad when she reached a chair because she wasn't sure she could stay on her feet any longer.

The moment she sat, he leaned back and steepled his hands in front of him. His gaze didn't move from her.

"It seems we have a breach in communication around here."

She couldn't continue to look at him and dropped her gaze to study her hands. "I guess so."

"Miss Dayton," he barked, "I *know* Russell contacted you. I was in the room when he made the call."

She looked at him again, but this time with a glare. "And were you in mine when I got his call? How was I supposed to know Mr. Arthur would come to get me?"

"You thought it would be me?"

"I did."

"And what led you to believe that?"

She watched him a moment, then shrugged. She'd simply assumed he would be her date; she'd assumed he would want to see her. What a foolish idea! She knew his opinion of models.

"I have other things to do than chauffeur you around, Miss Dayton."

"I know that."

"But still you thought any time you had to make an appearance, I would be available to escort you." He picked up the pen again. "It's flattering to know you wanted me to be with you, and I'm sorry to have disappointed you, but no matter who I decide your escort will be, that's who it will be. Your cooperation is guaranteed by the contract, I believe. The third clause, not the last one: 'You will make yourself available to represent Merchand.'"

"I didn't want you to escort me," she said. "I wasn't disappointed."

"Is that right?" He raised his eyebrows. "Well, that disappoints me because, you see, I had planned to take you last Saturday, but something came up at the last minute and I had to ask Shelby to fill in for me."

"I wouldn't have gone with you."

"You didn't go with Shelby," he said as if, had he been there, things would have worked out differently.

"But I offered to get ready."

"You had plenty of advance notice, Miss Dayton. From now on when you're requested to represent our company, I expect you to do exactly that—whether or not it's me who arrives to take you."

"Yes, sir. I understand. That clause is in the contract."

"It is. I warned you the day you signed that you might have objections. You raised none. It's a bit late in the game to think of them now—you've been launched as the Merchand Girl. And," he said firmly, "I fully expect you to bring your best efforts to your job."

Her hands clenched into fists. Except for that one lapse, she had given Merchand her best. "I will."

Derrick dropped the pen with a sudden clatter and looked as if something had just come clear to him. "You're not afraid to go out with me, are you, Miss Dayton?"

Her eyes narrowed and she didn't speak.

"My, my." He smiled as if he'd been paid a high compliment. "I told you I don't attack women; I don't seduce them either."

"I didn't think so," Pat flared. "I'd guessed you let them do that to you."

He considered the idea. "In your case I think I will, Miss Dayton. Yes, I think I will."

She jumped to her feet. "You egotistical man. I wouldn't dream of it."

"If I recall correctly, I told you it was all right for you to dream."

Pat turned her back to him and headed for the door.

"Miss Dayton!"

She stopped as if she'd hit an invisible shield.

"You're cute when you're angry," he said. There was a hint of laughter in his voice. "But I'm not finished with you."

She swung to look at him. "What else?" she shouted. The man would drive her to distraction. Or murder.

"A nationwide tour is in the works. When the television campaign begins, you'll make personal appearances at major department stores in many of the larger cities."

"So?"

"So I wanted to warn you ahead of time so you wouldn't be caught at the last minute. I didn't want a snarl in communications." He paused. "You'll be disappointed to learn I won't be going with you."

"Oh!" She'd kill him.

"Ryan Murdock will have that chore." He took the cap off the pen. "You're dismissed, Miss Dayton." He went placidly to work.

Chore! Pat trembled with anger.

Derrick looked up innocently. "Something else?"

She wanted to tell him she was delighted he wouldn't be going on tour with her, but no words would come out of her mouth. Saying that would have been a lie anyway.

"Isn't Thaddeus waiting for you?"

She turned with a rush and ran to the door. If she didn't have so many bills, she'd throw her job in his face and let him sue her. But all she was worth at the moment were debts, she needed the job—it was a good one—and she hadn't been mistreated.

By the time she reached the dressing room she had made up her mind to be more professional than she had been. She would live up to every letter of every clause—including the last one. She wouldn't think about Derrick Merchand. And the next time anyone asked her to go out, she'd get permission and go.

"Let's get busy," she said to Thaddeus.

When she went before the camera, Pat drifted into fantasy. Her dream lover was disturbingly similar to Derrick, so she concentrated on the man on the beach and let him take over more fully than he ever had. He was safer and less troubling.

Chapter Nine

After the stills were done, Patricia had a few free days before they were to begin television commercials. She spent some time catching up on rest, then her friend Jerry Phillips phoned and invited her to a concert. She didn't want to explain that she had to ask permission, so she told him she'd find out if she had any commitments at Merchand. She'd ring him back.

She called the offices and told the receptionist who Jerry was and where they planned to go. Mrs. Kelsoe asked her to hold for Merchand. Pat's clutch on the phone would have broken it had it been made of weaker plastic. She heard a few clicks, then Derrick said, "Yes?"

"I want to go out."

"Are you asking me for a date?"

She could almost see him lounging back in his chair. "No, I'm not. Jerry Phillips wants to take me to a concert."

"He does, does he? And does he know you're madly in love with me?"

Pat pulled the receiver from her ear, looked at it, then slammed it onto its hook. She wasn't in love with Derrick.

Three seconds passed before the phone rang. Some-one other than Merchand could be calling, but she let it ring six times before she picked it up, and then she didn't say anything.

"I'm afraid you'll have to tell me more about the man than his name."

She nearly hung up again. She hated having to ex-plain to Derrick. But she hadn't been anywhere in so long, she was going stir crazy. "He's a graduate student in psychology at Columbia," she said. This was like having to tell her father, tell how nice the boy was: *Yes, Daddy, he'll have me back by ten,* she thought.

"Um. And where did you say you planned to go?"

"To a concert in the park." Then dryly, "It's a *free* concert." *It won't cost you any money, Daddy.*

"What kind of music?"

"Bluegrass."

"Um. Hold on a second, Patricia." There was silence a long time and she had no idea what he was doing. "Pardon the interruption," he said. "Now. This con-cert, the bluegrass concert, is it casual?"

"Of course it's casual. What did you expect? That we'd wear formal dress to sit on the grass and listen to banjo pickers?"

"Where you're concerned, Miss Dayton, I've given up trying to know what to expect." He paused. "I'm afraid you can't go with Mr. Phillips."

She sputtered. "Why not? I asked you. You said I had to tell where I was going and who with."

"I never said you'd be allowed to go."

Pat was overwhelmed at his obstinacy. Perhaps the event wasn't elegant enough for the Merchand Girl. "If it was to an *opera*, would I be allowed to go?"

"That all depends. Do you want to go to an opera?"

"No," she shouted. "I want to go to the concert."

"Well, all right, then—if you insist. I've cleared my calendar and I can be there whenever you say. When does this bluegrass thing start?"

"I don't want to go with you. I want to go with Jerry."

"Afraid not. You either go with me or you don't go to the concert."

She didn't really, specifically, want to go to the concert; she just wanted to go somewhere, get work off her mind, relax. Evidently Merchand wasn't going to let her go anywhere without his supervision. Having to get out of his superb suits and sit on the grass would serve him right, show him things other than high executive levels of life existed. "What will Jerry think?" she asked.

"You needn't worry about Jerry. Mrs. Kelsoe is already taking care of your refusal."

"How?"

"She's calling the university to get his number from the student directory."

"I could have given it to you."

"You didn't."

"You didn't ask."

"Would you have given it to me if I had asked?"

"No."

"Well, then."

Pat hadn't told Derrick she wouldn't go with him; she hadn't even raised an objection when he said he'd have Jerry phoned. She looked at the phone again and wondered how she had let this situation develop.

"Miss Dayton, I have work to do. Tell me what time I should pick you up."

"Seven thirty."

"Very well. See you then."

She heard his phone rattle into place, and the hollow sound that came over the receiver had every bit as much intellectual content as her brain. She had to be crazy to have agreed to go with him.

When Pat got ready, she used Merchand cosmetics because there were no others on her dressing table any longer. She fluffed her hair the way Merchand liked it—there was little other way to wear it except bound in a turban. Then she put on sneakers, faded jeans and a flannel shirt. Derrick would probably hate the way she looked—he'd thrown such a fit about her coat. Tough shavings, she thought. She went into Becky's bedroom, where she was getting ready for her date with Morris.

"You can't go out with your boss dressed that way," her roommate said in dismay.

"Yes, I can. He knows where we're going. He didn't have to go with me."

"Why aren't you going with Jerry?"

"I couldn't. Merchand wouldn't let me. Jerry doesn't have enough high-and-mighty credentials, most likely. I'm going nuts having to work all the time and not go anywhere, and I had to go with Merchand or no one."

"Won't he fire you for dressing like that?"

"I don't think he can. I'm not doing anything he didn't royally grant permission for me to do." She crumpled suddenly onto the bed. "Oh, Beck, what am I doing?"

"What's wrong?" She sat and took Pat in her arms.

"I don't know why I said I'd go with him. I don't like him. I want to be with him and I don't want to be with him. I'm terrified of the man."

Becky smiled and leaned away. "Well, well. I do believe I detect a chink in your armor. You're interested
in a man."

"I'm not. I'm scared of him."

"Okay, you're not. But he's interested in you. He
wants to be with you."

"He *has* to be with me."

"I doubt that. He could have sent someone else or
let you go with Jerry."

Abruptly inspired, Pat looked at her friend. "Will
you do me a favor? Will you meet him when he comes
and tell him I'm sick? I have a terrible headache? I
broke a leg? I'm dying?"

"I won't tell the man anything. You can tell him you
are dying yourself."

"Becky, please."

"No. You'd never forgive me if I did."

"Traitor." She should have thought before she'd
submitted to going to the concert with him. She should
never have agreed because she remembered too vividly
how he had affected her the last time they went out
together. She should have thought before she signed
that damn contract.

The doorbell rang and Pat stiffened. She glanced at
the clock: twenty past seven. That could be Morris or
her boss.

"Will you get it?" Becky said from beneath the folds
of the dress she was putting on.

Pat looked at herself one last time, straightened her
shoulders, and took a couple of deep breaths. She told
herself to forget Derrick was her boss, to behave as if
he were a casual friend. She'd be polite and she
wouldn't think he was handsome or desirable.

When she opened the door, her resolutions dissolved like unbaked merengue in the rain. He was in a knit shirt and jeans, and the clothes fit him as if he'd been born to model them. A denim jacket, caught with one finger, was slung over his shoulder. If anything, he looked more delectable than he did in suits or fancy dress.

"Hi," he said.

"Hello."

"You know," he said, "It wouldn't be a bad idea if we did a couple of spots with you in jeans, not everything silk and velvet and chiffon. Appeal to the younger crowd and the urban cowboy types." He nodded: it had been decided. "With you on a horse or leading one. Do you ride?"

"I never have."

"Doesn't matter." He glanced at her waist and hips. "Turn around."

As if programmed, she whirled her back to him. "Well?" she asked over her shoulder.

"You'll do."

Before she could gather a retort, he looked beyond her. "Who is this gorgeous creation?"

Becky was dressed in her red dinner gown. It was the best one she owned, and set off her dark hair and fair skin.

"This is my roommate, Rebecca Cloud. Beck, this is Derrick Merchand."

He went past Patricia to take Becky's hand. "The man you have a date with is a lucky fellow. You're lovely."

"Thank you," Becky said, beaming.

Patricia folded her arms and glared at him. No wonder other women fell all over him; he could turn on the charm at will. He'd never done it to her. Instead he was arrogant and critical of her, or blatantly on the make. But she wasn't a woman to him, she was an employee, a model. When he gave her special attention, it was to make her feel like a naughty child or a seductress. She was neither of those.

He and Becky moved to sit on the couch, and Becky was saying "Pat has told me so much about you."

"Has she?" Derrick glanced at Patricia and raised an eyebrow.

"Yes," Becky said. "She loves her job with your company. But I'm worried about her. She never goes out. I don't think she's been three places in three months."

"She's been three places?" He looked at Becky again.

"I think that's all. She went for her introduction as the Merchand Girl, but I guess that was part of her job, so it doesn't count. And she went to dinner once." She stopped. "I guess she's only gone out twice, and one of those was for work."

"Twice," he said. "Do you think she wants to go out? She hasn't said so."

"She does. I know she does. But she hates to ask."

Pat wanted to sew her friend's mouth shut.

"Hates to ask," Merchand repeated. "Well." He looked a trifle uncomfortable as he got up. "It was nice to have met you, Rebecca."

Becky's dimples showed as she smiled at him, and she looked even prettier than she had earlier. "It was nice to have met you too, Derrick." She glanced at Patricia as if to ask why she'd ever said anything disparaging about him.

Pat narrowed her eyes. She knew the next time she and Becky were alone she'd be asked how she could complain about him, and she'd have to listen to how wonderful he was. But Becky didn't have the man in a position to tell her everything to do, nearly every breath to take.

Derrick was beside her again. "Have you got a jacket?" he asked. "It's still too chilly to be without one."

It might not be too late to chicken out. "We don't have to go," Pat said.

"I think we do. Rebecca was just telling me how unhappy you are staying cooped up all the time. Where's your coat?"

"It's the same one."

He smiled. "We haven't straightened out that snag yet, have we? Well, you'd better get it."

Now her coat was a snag. She got the snag and put it on.

When they reached the sidewalk, Derrick said, "I didn't bring my car. Shall we get a taxi, do we take the subway, or do you want to walk?"

Pat looked at him curiously. He wouldn't have room in his jeans for a subway token, much less a wallet to hold enough money for a taxi. "You decide," she said. He would anyway.

"How much time do we have?"

"Thirty minutes give or take. But we don't have to be punctual; there isn't an opening curtain. It's casual."

"Then let's walk." He slipped on his jacket and zipped it, then reached for her hand. She didn't give it to him, and he shrugged as if he were content without it.

When they crossed streets, his hand touched the small of her back protectively, possessively. But that was only a natural reaction and nothing more; she was a valuable commodity to him.

The music had started and they had to sit on the fringes of the crowd. Derrick took off his jacket, spread it out for her, then sat beside her with his knees tepeed in front of him and his arms draped around them as if he spent half his time lounging on the grass. He listened to the music as if he found it as satisfying and engrossing as a symphony, occasionally leaning toward her to make a comment about a tune or a technique. He didn't behave as if the evening were any different from dozens of others he'd spent, and maybe it wasn't. He seemed as much at home in the park as he did in his office. So much for putting him in his place. He was in his place no matter where he was.

At intermission he turned to her. "Have you eaten? Are you hungry?" Without waiting for her to answer, he pointed to a trolly. "I'll get us a hot dog." He got to his feet. "Orange or grape?"

"Hot dog?" Pat asked as though surprised they came in those flavors.

He grinned at her deliberate misinterpretation. "Drink."

She couldn't stop herself from smiling, and the ease of that made her begin to relax. "Cola."

"Gotcha." He mingled with the crowd around the refreshments, but he was easy for her to spot: he stood out as if he had a klieg light trained on him to follow his every step. Pat turned to study the crowd scattered along the grass. What was so hypnotic about Derrick Merchand? He was her boss. He was bossy. He directed her life whether or not she was working. And she didn't like the way he made her feel; she'd never been so aware of anyone before.

She glanced toward the food wagon again and found him immediately; he was coming toward her, loaded with drinks and hot dogs. "I got three dogs," he said when he reached her, "so if you want more than one, we can split the spare." He sat beside her and began to eat. "There's nothing like a park hot dog," he said with his mouth full. "I think they're the best in the world."

Derrick was like a kid on an outing, she thought as she ate. Nothing about him since they'd got to the park had been domineering, he relaxed and fit in as if he did things like this every day.

After he finished his first dog, he held the extra toward her. "Share?"

"No, thanks. One is enough for me."

"You're sure?"

"Yes." She smiled. "I can't let myself gain weight. Remember?"

"Or lose it," he said.

By the time he finished the second hot dog, the music had begun again. He took her napkin and cup with his and went to put them in a trash can. When he came back, he lay down with his head in her lap. "Mind?" he asked after the deed was already done.

She did and she didn't. The feel of his head in her lap was too intimate.

"You have a nice lap," Derrick said, and snuggled his head more comfortably into place. "You'll have to take me to the park more often."

Pat pretended to become engrossed in the music, but she didn't have any idea what the group was playing. She tried to concentrate on the sound and heard only a series of disconnected notes. The nearness of Derrick made her nervous. And when she was nervous, she fidgeted. She caught herself twisting a strand of his hair between her fingers. She jerked her hand away.

"Don't stop," he said. "That felt good."

She couldn't bring herself to do it when she knew she was doing it. She looked at him, and he smiled.

"I'm just a man," he said softly.

Pat wanted to tell him he wasn't just a man. She leaned back with her arms angled behind her and rested her weight on her palms. "I know."

"No, you don't."

She wasn't going to let herself think of him as a man. He was her boss. He was using her to promote his business. She wasn't going to give any of herself to him: not trust, not anything. She'd given trust and affection to Bart and had learned her lesson. Business was business.

So what was she doing in the park with Merchand? With his head on her lap? "I think we'd better go," she said.

"They aren't through playing yet."

"I've had a busy week. I'm tired. I think we'd better go."

Derrick didn't protest; he got up, took her hand, and helped her to her feet. "Too tired to walk home?"

It wasn't more than a dozen blocks. "No."

He leaned to get his jacket, shook it to get rid of loose blades of grass, then put it on. Again they walked side by side, not touching except when they crossed the street. They were like friends—comfortable with each other. But Patricia was too conscious of his stride; she found her steps matched his and deliberately changed cadence so they wouldn't. He adjusted his to be with hers again.

At her apartment building she didn't try to keep him

from coming to her door with her; he would anyway. She wondered what he'd do when they got there, remembering the last time he'd kissed her good night.

Outside her door Derrick stood to the side as she fished out her key. When she had it in her hand, she glanced at him.

"Good night, Patricia." He leaned toward her and touched his lips to hers, then sauntered away, leaving her wanting more of his kiss than that.

Chapter Ten

If Patricia thought the sessions she had gone through for the still photographs were draining and difficult, she found they had been nothing. In the television ads she had to get everything letter perfect: words, movements, expressions. Doing this type of ad, she had more difficulty dropping into fantasy to get proper expressions because she was eternally having to repeat dialogue.

Some of the commercials were filmed in the studio, but most were done on location. The crew covered a large part of the northeast, shooting in city, mountain, farm, gracious home, ranch. Two of the ads featured her in jeans and with a horse. The horse was beautiful and, fortunately for her, well trained: all she had to do was sit in the saddle.

On a typical day she would report at the scheduled time and if the work was to be done in a studio, she would be fluffed and groomed; if they were to go on location, she piled into the minibus with Florence and Thad, and after they arrived at their destination, she was fluffed and made up. The photographers, crew members, director, producer, and other cast members came by other conveyances.

Pat generally had her lines down—she never had many of them—and when she reported on the set, they had a run-through or two when the director specified moves he wanted made, named the expressions he desired, and suggested ways to phrase the lines. Problems escalated in proportion to the number of extra people involved. Everyone had to do the right thing at the right time.

After the preliminary directions, there were rehearsals, and then the shooting began. The designer or her representative was nearby to be sure Patricia looked bandbox perfect, and a cosmetologist was on hand to keep her face and hair absolutely correct. Sometimes a retake was necessary because the wind tossed her hair the wrong way or blew her dress into unflattering lines; sometimes she or someone else flubbed a line; sometimes the light wasn't right. More time was spent waiting around for things to get right than in actual work, but Pat had to be present and perfect every second. Occasionally a few seconds of a take would be ideal and could be edited in, clipped to other great seconds; but the director wanted everything to be flawless, and repeat takes were the order of the day.

Merchand showed up at most of the sessions and, except in one particular case, he didn't interrupt and didn't stay long. But one of the commercials was scheduled to be done on a deserted beach; there was to be a sunset scene with the backdrop of stained sky behind the Merchand Girl. When they began in late afternoon, he was there. He became tremendously picky and interfered with the professionals. Pat thought each take was as good as any other she'd done anywhere else, but nothing satisfied Derrick: the color wasn't right, her makeup, the lighting, her clothes, the action of the waves, her hair. He went to the city for the night and came back the next day. They had to repeat and repeat and repeat, day after day. Patricia began to think nothing existed except sunset and water. And though she wore a dozen different outfits—at Derrick's command—not one of them pleased him. He never approved any of the finished rushes; the beach advertisement was finally scrapped.

Pat always became acutely aware of him when he came to the set or the location, and she stayed that way until he left. When he was around, she couldn't fantasize. It wasn't possible; it wasn't necessary. She didn't want to be keyed to his presence or his actions, but she couldn't help herself. He fascinated her utterly.

During the months they were making TV ads she didn't think of a social life; she didn't have time, and when she did find time, she preferred to be alone. Becky pestered her to get Merchand to take her out again, but she wouldn't and he didn't phone. And Pat didn't want to be with anyone but him.

When the introductory batch of commercials were finally complete, Derrick called her to his office. Pat hadn't been alone with him since the evening in the park and was curious about what he'd say, how he'd behave. But she wasn't alone with him—Ryan Murdock was there. They sat in the casual corner of the office as Merchand outlined their scheduled tour, naming cities and stores they would visit: Murdock would coordinate; one of Thaddeus's assistants would go along to keep her up-to-the-minute groomed; she would be expected to be at cosmetic counters a part of each day, attend dinners and luncheons, make herself available for news interviews, and be on local television and radio shows. During the conference the only personal note from Derrick came when he said her wardrobe would be provided. He glanced at her, smiled, and said since it was warm weather, she wouldn't need a coat.

When the session was over and she and Murdock were leaving, Merchand said, "Would you stay a minute, Patricia?" He looked at her seriously with sincere appreciation and hope in his eyes. "You've done a fine job, Pat. We're going to make a go of this thing." He sighed. "I think."

Pat hadn't known he had doubted for a second. He had seemed sure of himself, as if because he wanted success, he'd have it. The fact that the cosmetic industry was one of the most difficult to break into and conquer hadn't seemed to bother him. "You will," she said. "Merchand puts out a good product. As good or better than anything on the market."

"If we succeed, you'll have been the element that made it possible." Derrick cocked his head. "I still wonder what it is you think about to give you such marvelous expressions."

You, she wanted to shout, *half the time it's you.* "I just dream."

He watched her a moment. "I'd go with you on this tour if I could. But I've already spent so much time on the new cosmetic line, I've let other things slide, and I can't neglect them any longer." He looked almost as if he were apologizing, asking permission to stay behind. "I have to work."

. His attitude was such a reversal, Pat was speechless. She unglued her tongue from the roof of her mouth. "All right."

Derrick went to his desk and began to fiddle with some papers. "Patricia?"

She waited for him to go on, but he didn't. "Yes?"

He glanced at her again, then abruptly became efficient, feigning interest in the papers he was shifting. "Do us proud. I'm counting on you."

"I'll do my best."

He gave her a strange expression and stopped his paper shuffling. "Of course you will. You're paid to do it, aren't you?"

She was his employee. He was pointing out that nothing personal existed between them. She drew herself erect. "Yes, I am. Am I dismissed?"

His hand was clenched on the desk and he put it carefully into his lap. "Yes, you may go."

As she left the office she thanked God she had a contract with the man. If she hadn't, the situation would have been more like her relationship with Bart—but Derrick would be more demanding than Bart had ever thought of being. And she'd be more willing. But he didn't think of her as anything but an investment, and she wouldn't think of him as anything but an investor.

On the tour Patricia scarcely had a chance to miss Derrick because he was so much with her in product, in essence, and in thought. She was waked in the morning to have Merchand makeup and perfume applied, her hair was kept trimmed and fluffed the way he wanted it, and she was constantly within sight of his name. When she was interviewed, she was asked about Merchand the company and Merchand the man. She could impart little information about Derrick, as she knew little about him—only that he could turn her on with a glance and she was wildly infatuated with him. She didn't say that. She outlined the work he did as far as she knew it. She spoke of him casually as a dedicated businessman who had aspirations and confidence, and spoke of his products as if they were the best in the world. She was the Merchand Girl with every tilt of her head, but with every thought in it, she wanted to be Merchand's girl.

At night when she went to bed, visions of him floated in her mind: the way he'd looked the first time she'd seen him, how gorgeous he had been dressed in his tuxedo, the sensuality of his movements when they danced, the way he had touched her back as they crossed streets on the way to the park, the comfortable way he lay with his head in her lap. Most vividly she remembered his kiss. She tried to make him go from her thoughts. She revived her fantasy lover and was partially successful, but only when she blended him with the man on the beach was she able to forget Derrick.

Pat thought she should go back to Otter Key and see if the fisherman was still there. He was what she needed; he'd wanted her with no name and no commitment. She let him take over her fantasies entirely; there hadn't been too much difference between him and her fantasy lover anyway. But still her sleep was filled with erotic dreams of Derrick Merchand.

She didn't see him for a month. He didn't come to any of the department store openings. He had said he wouldn't be at them because he'd neglected the other parts of his business, but she wished she could have seen him at least once, even though it wouldn't have made any difference, for she was determined not to give in to his sensuality. She wouldn't seduce him as he had said he would let her. *Let* her!

After they'd visited the major stores in what seemed

to be every city in the United States instead of just the large ones, they went home. Pat was so glad to be free of making appearances, she could have wept. The killing pace of the tour had exhausted her.

For nearly seven months she'd been working for Merchand and she needed a break—a real one—not just hiding in her apartment and having to ask for permission to go to the corner grocery store. She'd go to Rose's cottage. She bet Bubba hadn't seen a single one of the ads she'd done; he wouldn't be able to tell anyone where the Merchand Girl was because he wouldn't know she was it.

She'd go *if* Merchand gave permission. But he had said anytime she wanted to go to Otter Key all she had to do was ask and he'd approve.

Becky, bless her heart, was as vibrant and energetic as ever. She and Morris had set the date, and Pat was to be maid of honor.

"When is the wedding?" she asked.

"In a couple of weeks. We waited until after your tour because I wanted you to be there."

"I would have chucked the tour to be at your wedding."

"Sure!" Becky laughed. "You wouldn't have and you know it."

"Maybe you're right. Beck, you don't need me next week, do you?"

"I don't think so. Why?"

"I want to get away for a while. I'm bushed. I thought I'd go to Rose's cottage again."

"That's a great idea. You deserve a rest if anyone does. Can you be fitted for your dress first?"

Pat thought she'd probably been fitted enough to last a lifetime, but she said, "Easily."

"His folks and mine are coming here for the wedding. We couldn't decide whether to get married in his hometown or in mine, so we compromised." She laughed. "Neither. And that way all our friends will be able to come."

"Beck," Pat began. She wanted to ask if she'd ever desired Morris so much, she thought she'd die. But Becky's circumstances were different: she and Morris were friends, he wanted her too—and for more than an evening's playmate. "I think I'll go to bed early," she said lamely.

But she couldn't sleep. Until late in the night she tossed and turned, thinking that on the next day she'd get to see Derrick. And she'd have to be cool and composed—as if he meant nothing to her.

She finally slept, but her rest was fitful and she wakened early.

For the first time in weeks Patricia had to do her own face, and her fingers trembled so, she could barely get her lip line right. She was being foolish to let herself get in a tizzy. Other than her representing the corporation successfully, only one thing about her interested Derrick—and he might have given up his desire. He hadn't made a pass at her since their first outing.

When she went outside, she found a chill had moved in—the first of the season. Spring and summer had come and gone, and it was early autumn. She had been so busy during the past months, she hadn't had time to enjoy the gentle seasons.

The sky had a steel-gray, cold look; clouds without contour spread a dull expanse above the city, kept the sun from shining through, and offered nothing to replace the beauty they shielded. Tiny drops of rain began to fall: not big healthy drops that make quarters on the sidewalk, but insidious little wisps that wet the cement before one becomes aware it's raining. If Pat hadn't been so eager to see Merchand again, she would have stayed home. Everyone should stay home on a day like this.

She went inside for her raincoat and umbrella. The tires of the taxi spun as they drove off. There would be a number of fender-benders in the city today, as the light rain had floated oil to the surface and made the streets slick.

When she reached the executive office level and started across the reception room, Mrs. Kelsoe said, "Mr. Merchand isn't in, Miss Dayton."

Pat couldn't keep her disappointment from showing. "Where is he? I mean, when will he be back?"

"I'm not sure. You can ask Russell if you like."

The carrot-topped young man was typing. He glanced at her without stopping his fingers. "Damn," he said. "Sorry," he said immediately afterward, and nodded at the typewriter. "I made a typo. May I help you?"

"Mr. Merchand?"

"He had to go to Albany; something about a governmental contract for decorative metals. If you want to wait, he shouldn't be too long. He phoned this morning and said he was on his way back."

She didn't want to wait a second, but she knew she'd wait all day if she had to. "How long?"

Russell glanced at his watch. "If his plane was on time, he's already landed. He'll be back in less than an hour, I'd imagine. He had me cancel only his appointments before eleven, so I'm sure he assumed he'd be here by then."

"I'll wait."

"You can wait in his office if you wish. He said if you

showed up, he wanted to see you. He has been working on the next campaign and I think he wants your opinion."

Of course work would be why he wanted to see her. "I'll wait in there."

Without him, his office was barren: a hollow room that didn't hold anywhere near enough of his personality to satisfy her. She wandered to his desk, went behind it, and let her fingers run across the back of his leather chair. She looked at the papers scattered on the desktop and wondered if he knew where anything was in that jumble. She looked at the prints on the walls, the books in the low bookcase, then want to stare out the window at the gray haze that blanketed the city. She sat on the padded bench and thought of the time she'd been there with him; before she'd signed the contract, before he owned her. But he owned more than he'd ever wanted, more than the contract specified, more than he knew. He owned most of her waking thoughts and all her sleeping ones. Which clause covered that? she wondered.

Pat thought perhaps she should visit Florence while she waited. She hadn't seen the woman in over a month, and the clothes she had fashioned had been appreciated at every stop on the tour. And Thaddeus could be in the dressing room. But if she went, maybe Derrick would come and she'd miss him. She tried to tell herself she didn't have to see him on his absolute first appearance in the office. She didn't actually have to see her boss at all, she could have phoned for permission to go to Rose's cottage. But she didn't leave; she *did* have to see him. More than she'd ever had to do anything, and she didn't want to delay seeing him a minute longer than was necessary.

The door opened and Derrick came in. "Patricia," he said, smiling at her. "Russell said you were in here." He took off his hat and shook rain from it. "Beautiful day, isn't it?"

"Yes. It is." At that moment it was. Then she realized he was being facetious. "I mean, no, it's miserable out."

He took off his coat and went to hang it and the hat on a coat tree in the corner. "Winter will be here before we know it." He turned to her and was quiet a second, then he went toward his desk. "You did a good job on the tour; all the reports were favorable, and the sales are unbelievable. If things go on as they are, within two years we'll be one of the dominant names in the business." He shifted a few papers and drew one out. "Listen to this. We outsold Chanel and Arpège and Max Factor. In fact, during the past month we outsold everyone in the perfume business."

"You put out a good fragrance."

Derrick let the paper flutter to the desk. "The Christmas season hasn't even begun yet, and we'll really shove our wedge in then. We have to do some special Christmas ads—winter scenes. Do you ski?"

"I have. Once."

He waved his hand. "Doesn't matter. You just have to stand on the skis."

"Like I had to sit on the horse."

"Yes. Like that." He shut up suddenly and stared at her a few moments. "What do you do?" he asked.

"About what?"

"Sports. You don't ride, you don't ski; what do you do?" He paused. "We might be able to fit it into the campaign."

"I swim," she said, back in her place, giving information to the boss. For a second she had thought he was interested in her as a person, but he only asked so he would be able to improve the advertisements. "I can ice skate. I do yoga."

"Do you."

It wasn't a question, just a notification that he'd assimilated the facts. She wondered how she could sit so calmly. He'd never think of her as anything but a substructure on which to hang his products. He didn't even want her sexually anymore. He probably wouldn't believe her if she brought up the things he had said, the time he had teased her. "I want to take a break," she said.

"You deserve one. We can work it in."

"I want to go to my cottage in Florida for a while."

Derrick sat forward in his chair. "You do? That's a good idea. I'm going to take off a few days as well. We've both been working too hard. I think I'll take a trip too."

"Then it'll be all right?"

"Of course it will. When do you expect to leave?"

"Tomorrow morning."

"So soon?"

"I have to be back for Becky's wedding in a couple of weeks."

"She is," he said.

Patricia frowned. He wasn't listening to her. She hadn't said Becky was getting married in a couple of weeks, but that she had to be back for Becky's wedding. *She is* wasn't a sensible response from anyone who was listening. "Yes, she is," she said, on the edge of tears, but she made them go away. Pat didn't want to be in his presence any longer; in fact, she'd leave today and spend the night in Tampa. She'd leave a note for

Becky, and include measurements for her dress. With incredulity she realized this would be her first dress in over half a year that hadn't been selected by Merchand.

"So it's all right if I take off for a while?" she asked.

"Yes, yes, it's fine. Wonderful."

Derrick felt as if he'd been waiting years for her to say she wanted to go to the island again. He couldn't expect to have everything arranged for his absence until at least midday tomorrow. Two days from now he had a scheduled meeting with his pharmaceutical division director, but he'd postpone it. And the board meeting was next week—he'd miss it if he had to. He'd fly to Tampa, get his boat from the marina in St. Pete, and be on the island by tomorrow evening. He was going to be on Otter Key when she was, and there, where they'd be equal, with no employee–employer relationship between them, he'd be able to get her to see him as a man.

Derrick leaned back in his chair and looked at her. All he wanted to do was look at her and see how she was. He had missed her. If anything, she was more beautiful and desirable than he remembered. He had been so blasted busy, he hadn't had time to follow up on any of his instincts about her. He had scared her off with his early rush on her and now wished he hadn't done that. But dammit, she exuded such appeal; she had to know she did, she put it out for the camera every time she sat before one.

Pat was just another model, he told himself—an extravagant, indiscriminate one. But he wanted her more than he'd ever wanted anyone. Looking at her wasn't enough; he wanted to touch her. Derrick wondered when she'd become more important to him than just as someone to play with. He was afraid it had been since the beginning on the beach when he'd held her in his arms. Suddenly, he didn't see her in the dress she had on, but in the shorts and tied-up blouse she had worn on Otter Key, and he smiled. He couldn't make himself stop smiling at her. He didn't know what was wrong with him. But he'd see her on the island, she'd learn he had been the man who had made her respond with such fire, and he'd make love to her this time. Beyond that, he didn't want to think. He wouldn't think of marriage. No one in his family married young; his father had been forty-two, his mother thirty-seven, and he was only thirty-five. But he *had* thought of it. Just then. His smile vanished; he grew thoroughly solemn and a little frightened. Oh, no, she couldn't! She wouldn't get him to the altar! He wasn't ready for a wife!

Patricia stood. "May I?" she asked.

"No. You may *not*!"

She sat back down. "What else, then?"

For a moment he was puzzled, then he realized she was talking business, asking for instructions. "Nothing now," he said. "You may go."

She headed for the door.

"Miss Dayton," he said, and when she looked at him, he smiled again. "Have a nice trip."

Chapter Eleven

The campaign had been more effective than Patricia realized: Bubba had seen ads for Merchand cosmetics and perfume. If he had, nearly everyone had. "You must be making lots of money," he said and grinned around his cigar. "But I'll be nice and not charge any more than I ever do."

"Thanks, Bubba. Is the new owner on the island?"

"Not as I know. He don't go from here; he has his own boat. Far as I know, hasn't been anyone over there since the last time you were here."

"Summer isn't exactly the best time of year for travel to Florida," Pat said. "It's warm everywhere. Perhaps the owners will come during winter. They could be snowbirds."

"Could be."

"Do they have electricity?"

"Yep. Brought a barge right in here and loaded a generator on to take it over. Maybe they'd let you tie in."

She laughed. "That's doubtful. But I can get along with the bare necessities.

"I don't even know why the fellow built the place. He coulda found something else to do with his money, unless he's so rich he can afford to throw it away." He gave Pat an irate look. "Imagine having a perfectly good house and not living in it."

"Well, Bubba, Aunt Rose's cottage might not be as fine, but it's livable, and I don't live in it."

"That's different. Rose did."

"True."

Rose's husband, Joe, had made his living oystering and had found Otter Key before he and Rose married. In spite of the primitive facilities, she'd agreed to live there with him because—and she continued to joke about her reasoning long after Joe died—it was closer to his work. Joe had to be up at the crack of dawn to go rake the bars and bottoms of the Gulf for oysters, and they went to bed when it was too dark to see. They'd had no real use for electricity. Rose had seen a few television shows, but had decided watching the changing color and movement of clouds and tides was more entertaining. Even after Joe died, she hadn't resorted to piped-in entertainment; she had still been content to watch the sea and sky.

Pat's mother and father had found each other; Rose had found Joe. Both of those couples enjoyed love and contentment with each other. Did such matches happen anymore? The world was different now, and it seemed no one ever found anyone for longer than a short relationship. Maybe Beck and Morris would be lucky, they seemed as much friends as lovers. and maybe that was a better foundation for marriage than was sexual compatibility. If one could have both, that would be unbeatable, but if one had to choose, friendship might have a more reasonable hope of survival. Pat was sure she'd never find either.

"No books this time," Bubba commented as he helped her load the boat.

"No. I didn't read half those I brought last time, so I didn't see any need to bring more. And lots of canned goods were left over. I'm traveling light this time."

"That's a matter of opinion," he said and nodded at her two suitcases and three bags of groceries. He started the engine for her. "See you when I see you."

Clouds were building up, and the waves were choppy with a wind from the north. Because of the conditions, Bubba had given her a larger boat this time, but he hadn't charged more than he would have for her usual sixteen-footer. She concentrated on keeping the bow of the boat straight so she wouldn't wallow. Had the bay between the island and the mainland been much more turbulent, she couldn't have made the crossing. Once she'd been stuck on the Key with her parents while a storm blew itself out, and right now she didn't care if she got stranded, as she didn't have anywhere to go.

It was barely past noon when Pat tied the boat to the dock so it would bump only against the worn tires that had been fastened along the sides. She got everything into the cottage and checked the stove—no more waiting until the last minute to do necessary chores. She heated some Campbell's vegetable soup and ate that with a peanut-butter sandwich. She put on shorts, a halter, and sneakers. The time before, she'd been afraid to walk to the opposite end of the island and see the new house because she'd thought she might run into the man from the beach. Chances were remote he'd be here this time, but if she saw him, she wouldn't be afraid of him.

As she cut through the gap in the trees she looked at the place where she had seen him and wondered if he would be able to make her forget Merchand.

After a few minutes of walking along the shoreline,

Pat took off her shoes and stuck them up on the beach where the tide wouldn't get them. A few sand dollars and some scallop shells were scattered along the sand, but she didn't save any of them. A complete collection of local shells was encased in glass on one wall of Rose's cottage, and none of the specimens she found was finer than the samples already there.

When she neared the far end of the island, she saw an opening, and after a few steps, a house. It was modern with planes going every direction. A skylight was in the roof. The house was made of unstained cedar, which was beginning to lose its natural pinkish hue and turn silver. The builder had shown meticulous regard for trees: in some places, less than a foot separated the walls of the house from the trunk of a large oak or pine. There was no formal lawn. As far as Patricia could tell, no grass had been planted. Cedar boardwalks had been built to reach from the porch to the shore on the north and west.

She went up the west walk. Windows covered most of the side and the front of the house, but drapes had been pulled and she could see nothing inside. The house was lovely. Beside it, Rose's cottage would look like a tar-paper shack, even though the little house was solidly built and was easily able to withstand hurricanes and keep out winter winds when they invaded this far south.

Pat made a circuit of the new house and found nothing about which to complain—it was perfect. It fit into the terrain and brought the terrain into it. She let her fingers trail over the wood of the wall before she left the porch. Whoever had built the house had loved the island, and if for no other reason, she would like them for that. Still, she couldn't help but feel selfishly glad they weren't here now. She had the entire island to herself. She didn't even have to share with the fisherman.

But on the way back to her cottage she looked for him in the brush and trees, looked to see if a boat was near. Nothing was in sight except a liner afloat on the tight wire of horizon.

At home, she put a lounge chair near shore, then made dinner and ate outside where she could see the hazy, distant spires of trees on the mainland and watch the distant boats on the now gentled swells of the sea. One of the boats, a sailboat, was going against the grain of the larger ones—going out. Perhaps it was an after-work sailor taking advantage of the breeze during the light that remained? As she watched he turned and began to tack toward shore. Poor fellow. Scarcely got away before he had to return.

"You'd go sailing with me even if it were only for a short space of time, wouldn't you?" her dream lover said. His voice was similar to Merchand's. But she didn't mind if he had a voice like Derrick's. He always had, hadn't he?

"I love you, Patricia." He wavered and lost his clothes and became the fisherman haloed in the roseate tint of dusk. She had forgotten to look at the sunset, and day was nearly gone. "Come to me. Come with me. I want to make love to you." He wavered again and became Merchand.

"No!"

Pat took her plate into the house and put it in the sink before she went out the back door to follow the path. When she got to the break between the trees, she saw the sun hadn't finished tracing its memory across the clouds.

The tree had no one beside it; the beach was bare. She sat on the soft sand just where it began to change character and become flat and damp. The water was yards away, ebbing. The last bits of color left the sky, and the blue that remained grew darker. A few stars came out, and there was barely any light. The evening air was cool on her skin—a touch—as if someone caressed her.

She glanced up the beach and saw a man coming toward her; she wasn't sure if it was her fantasy or the fisherman. She shut her eyes briefly, and when she opened them, he was still there, and she knew he must be the fisherman. She got up and hurried toward the shelter of trees.

"Wait!"

If she hadn't known better, she would have sworn that it was Derrick's voice. But she did know better. She dreamed of him so often and thought about him so much, even let her fantasy lover have his voice, no wonder the sound was the same. She went faster and had reached the path before he called again for her to wait.

The man could be someone who'd had boat trouble and thought she could call for help. She didn't have a phone, she couldn't help anyone, but the man wouldn't know that. He was most likely concerned about his shipwrecked state and wanted to get a message to the wife and kiddies. She should be civil.

She stopped and saw him come through the gap. He was only a silhouette, no feature of his face could be recognized, but he was built like the man she'd seen fishing. As he came nearer she knew he was the same; he smelled the same.

"You!" she said.

"Yes. It's me." He must have run the last distance; he was nearly out of breath.

With a sudden thrill she remembered how wonderful his arms had felt. "How did you know I'd be here?" she asked. "Or do you come every evening?"

He was quiet a few seconds. "I thought you recognized me."

"I do. You're the man who was fishing the last time I was here." With him she wouldn't be embarrassed as she would be if she threw herself at her boss and was rejected, and if she kissed this man again, maybe she'd be able to forget Merchand. She moved a step closer, trying to see his face in the night shadows and failing. "I thought you were joking when you said you'd see me again. How did you know I was back?" She touched his chest. "Are you a witch, or do you have psychic powers?"

"Neither," he said brusquely.

"Well," she murmured. "Here we are."

He grasped her arms. "You'd make love to me, wouldn't you?"

"I guess so." Who would be a better choice to relieve her frustrations? She didn't know this man; she didn't even know what he looked like. He was simply a male figure in the night.

"Do you know what you do to me?" he whispered as his mouth came down hard on hers.

Pat had forgotten the power of his kiss; she wasn't going to be able to be as cool about this as she'd thought. His tongue signaled he wanted entry, and she opened her mouth; he kissed her deeply and pushed her halter from her shoulders. With steady pressure he urged her to the ground, where one of his legs pinned both of hers and his hand traced the shape of her neck.

then moved to caress a breast. His lips touched the hollow at her throat, then drifted lower, tongueing her nipple until it was rigid, then taking it into his mouth. He played fleetingly with her navel and explored the conformation of her belly. His boldness strengthened and he caressed the outer shape of her thigh, then drew along the soft inner flesh. His tongue and mouth tormented her; his lips took leisurely advantage, moving slowly and with seductive brushes from one breast to the other.

His breath was warm on her skin, and the gentle suction of his mouth was erotic. Pat couldn't stop the animal reaction of her body; she needed him.

He unfastened the catch of her shorts. His mouth left her bosom and, with a series of kisses traveled downward to her navel. "You want me, don't you?"

On the lonely and distant tour Pat had thought she'd be able to make love with this stranger, but now she held back, and she knew why: Derrick Merchand. The only man she wanted to touch her was Merchand; the only man with whom she wanted to make love was Merchand. "No, I don't want you."

He let go of her shorts and his mouth met hers again. The fisherman kissed her slowly, sensuously, warmly—as if he loved her—and then the kiss opened into passion, making him groan. He drew away. "Damn. You make me so sad," he said. "You don't even know who I am."

"No." She tried to see him, but she couldn't. The night was much too dark.

He sighed, long and deep, rolled off her, and walked away. He was nothing but a sound until he got to the beach, where she could see his silhouetted shape against the deep blue-black of sea and sky.

Quickly, for fear that he might change his mind and
return—she had been so near capitulation—Pat felt for
her halter, found it, then went home along a path she
couldn't see.

As she struck a match to light the lantern, her fingers
shook. She couldn't stay on the island. The fisherman
might come back; the time before, she'd told him she
lived on Otter Key, and there were only two houses to
check. But she couldn't go home, she couldn't tell
Becky why she hadn't stayed for the week and, if Derrick learned she'd come back early, she certainly
couldn't explain to him.

She went to the window; the lights across the way
were hazed by a misty fog into faint gloss. The bay
wasn't as rough tonight as it had been earlier, and she
could steer using the glow from Bubba's landing as her
guide.

She threw her things haphazardly into suitcases and
made sure everything was shut down properly. She
wasn't sure when, or if, she'd ever come back.

Merchand had got halfway to this house before he
turned abruptly as if he'd forgotten something. He was
furious with Patricia. At first he'd thought she knew
who he was, but it had become evident she didn't. Still,
she'd been seductive, had wanted to make love. And
he had wanted her. She wasn't to be trusted. Twice in
that same spot she'd teased him until he was almost
crazy with need. He had wanted her so badly, he almost
hadn't been able to stop himself—until the last second
he hadn't known if he could leave her. He hated her for
being eager with a stranger on the beach when she had
put him off so primly in New York. He should have
gone on. Pat wanted him even though she denied it,

but he wouldn't satisfy her—he wanted her to know who he was when he finally made love to her. Derrick realized he clutched a pine cone in his fist. He stopped long enough to hurl it into the Gulf, then he found the path and followed it until he could see light coming from the windows of her cottage.

He leaned against a tree and debated going in and facing her with the fact that it had been he on the pine needles with her, he she had touched so wonderfully when she had first seen him, he she had refused.

The light went out. He heard her around front and went quietly to see what was happening. Pat locked the door and with two suitcases went onto the dock that in broad daylight looked too unstable to trust. She lowered the bags into a boat, then got in herself. After a few false starts, the engine caught and the boat moved away from the Key.

He made his way to the end of the dock and sat to watch her boat as it dwindled into the darkness of the span between the island and the mainland. Only a tiny glimmer of running lights told him where she was, and even that became unsure as she neared the opposite shore. He lay back on the boards of the dock and looked at the sky. Fog had obliterated the stars, and only a film of light showed that a moon was behind there somewhere.

Patricia couldn't be trusted. He would have to watch her; keep her out of someone's arms, someone's bed. As long as she was the Merchand Girl, Derrick could keep her straight. He didn't want her any longer, but he sure as hell didn't want the image of his company cheapened by the sexual shenanigans of its most visible representative. Sure she had put him off toward the end both times he had tried to make love to her, but she'd begun things both times. If he had been anyone else, he wouldn't have stopped.

He should have gone on.

Derrick smashed his fish against a piling that rose above the level of the dock. All he got for the effort was bleeding knuckles and a sudden stab of pain that made his inner ache ebb for a fraction of a second.

He stayed the night and in the morning he walked the beach. He found her shoes on the shore and, with fury, threw them as far out into the surf as he could. He wondered how many men she had been with, whom she had loved, what she had done before he met her.

She had left the Key—gone back to New York. He would return as well and ask her the questions that were plaguing him. But he wasn't sure he wanted to hear the answers.

Chapter Twelve

"What's going on?" Becky asked Patricia when a week later she returned to New York. "Mr. Merchand's secretary has called every day since the one after you left. You're supposed to report to him the minute you show your face."

"I'm supposed to report to Russell?" Pat joked, and smiled at Rebecca. She knew who wanted to see her; she didn't know why he wanted to see her, but she knew why she wanted to see him.

"No, not Russell. Mr. Merchand wants to see you."

Pat glanced at the clock on the little imitation mantel. "I'll have to wait until tomorrow. It's almost seven, no one will be in the office at this hour."

"Don't count on it." The phone rang. "Right on cue," Becky said. "This is usually when Russell phones: after I'm home from work and before I have a chance to go out." Becky picked up the receiver, listened, and nodded at Pat. "Just a moment." She covered the mouthpiece. "I told you. He wants to talk to you."

Pat took the phone. "Yes?" she said, not sure whether Russell or Derrick would be on the line. It was Russell. "You've been trying to get in touch with me?" she asked.

"I have." His voice was tense and haggard. "Merchand is in a rage. I've never seen him so disturbed. Get down here."

"But it's after hours."

"Tell that to him. I've had to stay late every night if for no other reason than to try to locate you. He'll be here until at least nine."

"What does he want?"

"Don't ask me. Just get down here and get that man off my back. We've done a month's work in a week. We've caught up on everything—things that have been backlogged for a year. I can't take any more." He hung up.

Pat looked at the phone a second, then replaced it. "What the devil?"

"What did he say?" Becky asked.

"Just to get down there. Something must have gone wrong with the campaign. He said Mr. Merchand was angry and was working him to death."

"Then I guess you'd better go."

"I haven't been away but a week. I wonder what could have gone wrong."

"You won't find out standing here asking me, 'cause I sure don't know! But I'd like to, so hustle on down there, then you can tell me and we'll both know."

Her boss's anger could have been caused by anything. A fire could have broken out and burned copies of the advertisements and they needed to be replaced in a rush. But that didn't seem likely; something like that would have reached the Orlando papers and she would have learned of it. Had the sales dropped unbelievably because of her ads? That didn't seem likely either. They were the same ads that had caused the surge in sales.

It was strange to be in the building after hours; the night watchman was the only person on the lower floor. He had her sign in. She was alone in the elevator, the receptionist's desk was vacant, and Russell's office was empty. When Pat opened the door to Merchand's office, he was pacing. His jacket was off, his tie was pulled loose, and his hair looked as if he'd raked his fingers through it dozens of times.

When she stepped into the room, Derrick stopped and glared at her. "So you decided to come back," he said harshly.

For a moment she was taken aback. Was he angry with *her*? "Well, yes. My week was just over."

"Where have you been?"

He could have needed to get in touch with her and sent someone to Otter Key to locate her—and she hadn't been there. "I went to Disney World."

"Disney World," he repeated as if the taste of the words fouled his tongue. Then he shouted, "You had permission to go to your cottage. Nowhere else."

"I—"

"You did *not* have permission to go to Disney World."

It had never crossed her mind he'd object. Truthfully, it had never crossed her mind he'd find out. "Something came up," she said.

"Something did, did it?" His eyes narrowed. "You aren't to be trusted a second, are you?"

"Yes, I am."

"You've proved that! The first chance you get, the first time you're away from my orders, and you behave like that."

"It was only Disney World. I had no idea you'd object to a family attraction."

"The fact remains that you didn't have permission to go anywhere other than Otter Key."

"Well, I did and I'm back. What did you want to see me about?"

Derrick didn't answer, he just looked at her as if she were a cretin; then he turned his back—she was unworthy of his attention—and went to his desk.

"Are you going to *fire* me for going somewhere without asking permission?"

"I could, you know." He slumped into his chair, raked his hair, and looked at her. "Do you think I had those clauses added as a joke? I knew when I first looked at you that you weren't to be trusted."

"I am to be trusted. I didn't know you'd be so determined to stick to the precise letter of your law. I was in Florida. You said I could go to Florida."

"What else have you done without letting me know? Did you have a lot of late-night flings when you were on tour with Murdock? I wasn't there to keep you in line."

How dare he! "What if I did?" Pat shouted. "You don't own my body—just my work and my loyalty to your company. That's all."

"Part of your responsibility to the company is to keep a respectable image. You can't even do that."

"I can and I have."

"Can you? Have you?" Derrick was off his chair and beside her. He took her arms and yanked her to him. His mouth came fiercely down on hers.

Pat had wanted him to hold her again, but not like this—not in anger. She pushed away. "Don't."

"Don't?" A short laugh, like that of a madman, came from him. "Don't?" Almost thoughtfully his lips touched her brow, moved to close one eye, then slid to touch the edge of her lips. "Don't?" he asked again. His mouth covered hers softly, sweetly, not demanding, but asking; moving back and forth against hers, making her dreams of him come again, making the other times he'd held her return as near as now. Making her think of the fisherman.

"Don't?" he said against her lips, and she took the breath of the word into her mouth and wanted more.

Derrick held her away so he could look at her. That infernally seductive expression was on her face, like it was in her pictures. This time she was thinking of him. How about all the other times?

His mouth touched hers again and his arms slipped beneath hers to wrap around her and make her put her arms over his shoulders. Pat gave herself to his kiss completely, quested with her tongue before he asked. He pressed her to him and knew she'd feel how she affected him. He'd have kept from betraying his desire if he could have, but his hand betrayed him, too, and went to cradle her breast.

Patricia wanted him madly. She made a low sound in her throat, and he raised his head to look into her eyes.

"You'd make love to me, wouldn't you?" he asked. "This time you'd say yes."

"Yes," she breathed.

Derrick put her from him abruptly and smiled cruelly. "You're to be trusted? I can see that."

She flamed with embarrassment. She had known he would be this way if she threw herself at him. She hated him for arousing her, for making her want him, for being in her thoughts at all. She wanted to hurt him as badly as he'd hurt her. "Sorry," she said flippantly. "Sometimes it's difficult to control physical responses. My weakness had nothing to do with you."

His face paled. "No?" He grabbed her arms again. "Any man would do! That's so, isn't it? That's why I have to watch you, to keep you from tarnishing the image of Merchand's girl."

"Not Merchand's girl," she said softly, and her heart broke. "*The* Merchand Girl."

He looked as if she had slapped him.

"I won't cheapen the image," she said.

"You're damn right you won't. I'll watch you every minute if I must."

They glared at each other. Derrick had rejected her so thoroughly, she wanted to die, but she couldn't die, she had to live—and living hurt horribly. With a disdainful lift of his lip he broke the eye contact and went behind his desk. He sat and fiddled with some of the clutter on his desk, obviously trying to calm himself. Finally, he looked at her again.

"We have some new commercials to do, new magazine spreads," he said flatly with no feeling. "They have to be done quickly to meet the Christmas deadline. And there is another tour scheduled."

She had thought the next time she saw him would be so different. "All you think about is business, isn't it?"

"At least I know how to handle that."

"Why don't you just fire me?"

His lips thinned. "I think only about business, remember? Hundreds of thousands of dollars have been invested in you, and it would be a waste to let that go to hell. You photograph well. You have been launched to represent us." His eyes turned cold. "Maybe we can stick it out for the rest of the contract. Maybe I can keep you out of everyone's bed for that long."

"I quit," she yelled. "I don't hop into everyone's bed."

"No?" he asked cynically. "I guess that's because the men have control."

She reddened as she remembered the man on the beach had stopped, and Merchand had pushed her away when she said yes. She started toward the door, rigid with anger and bereft with loss.

"Patricia," he said sharply.

"I don't work for you anymore. I just quit."

"You can't. You won't work for anyone ever again if you do. I'll have your name removed permanently from every list in this country and in Europe."

Pat whirled toward him. "You couldn't."

"I could and I would. You'd never work as a model again. And despite the fact you have a lovely and expressive flair for theater, as you so clearly showed in your speech from *Romeo and Juliet,* you couldn't get a job acting either. I can fix that as well."

"I chose an apt speech, didn't I?" She was half an inch from tears. "I had no idea how appropriate it was."

"It was appropriate, wasn't it? For you. Your angel face belies the devil you keep inside." He cocked his head at her. "I know another speech, one more appropriate, perhaps, from *Hamlet*, about how Gertrude rushed from one husband to another."

"I've never been married. Much less twice."

"That's true. But you do hurry from one man's arms to another's. At least that's what you try to do."

Furious, she opened her mouth to ask how he knew anyone save him had held her, but she snapped it shut without speaking. The fisherman could still have been on the island, and whoever Merchand sent to find her could have spoken with him and he could have told when and how he had seen her. She turned red with embarrassment as she visualized the man saying he'd touched her, fondled her. But nothing had happened. And, anyway, that episode was none of her boss's business. "I don't dash from one man to another, but I can see you'll never believe me."

"Right," he said dryly. "You'd never know the difference."

"About what?"

"About anything."

She'd had enough of this. "May I go now, *Mr. Merchand*, or are you not quite through raking me over the coals?"

"I'm through for now, *Miss Dayton*. Be here at seven in the morning. Thaddeus will be waiting."

"Yes, *sir*."

She slammed the door behind her with all the force she could muster. It made a satisfying crash. And she was home before she realized she hadn't learned why he had wanted to find her. He had spent all the time she was with him chastening her and putting her solidly in her place.

Becky and Morris were waiting at the apartment when she returned. "Well?" Becky said. "What was it all about?"

Pat shrugged. "I went to Disney World without asking permission."

"I thought you went to your aunt's cottage."

"I did, but I decided to go to—oh, forget it. He was angry with me, that's all."

"He didn't fire you?"

"No. He didn't fire me."

The next day, not one minute after Pat met Thaddeus, Merchand came into the room. As usual, she hadn't bothered with makeup and her hair was in a turban. Derrick glanced at her with a studied lack of expression, and she wondered if he would tell her she couldn't cross the city looking the way she did. He didn't; he said, "Morning, Patricia." Then he told Thad he wanted final approval of her and to let him know when she was ready.

This was a day for stills, so she had no words to learn. She was glad; if she'd had to tell people to buy Merchand products, she would have screamed her lines and said if they didn't he would surely kill her.

The pictures today were to promote a night cream. Pat was put in a beautiful flowing peignoir—the kind of outfit women in horror films always wore when the monster carried them off into the swamp. Before Pat was moved to the studio, Merchand was called. He looked at her in the diaphanous gown and said, "That won't do."

"But, Mr. Merchand," Florence said. "You chose it."

"Perhaps so. But I don't choose to use it now. Put some clothes on her."

"She looks wonderful," Thaddeus added.

Merchand glared at him. "Yes, she does. But we don't want our product bought only by women in bordellos, now, do we?" He turned to Florence. "It's a beautiful getup, and my objection has nothing to do with the design. I just don't want her in it."

Florence was at a loss. All the costumes for the layouts had been approved by Merchand long ago. "Then, what?" she asked.

"Try some pajamas."

An amused smile curved her bright red lips. "Pajamas?"

Derrick scowled. "Why not? Merchand products are different; they offer a new approach to skin care and beauty. Why can't our ads reflect that? Get her some pajamas."

"But we haven't designed any."

"Then go buy some."

Patricia knew he was behaving unreasonably to make her feel small. "Do you want me to wear pigtails?"

Derrick shot her a glance "No. I like your hair the way it is."

He thought she looked beautiful, but he'd thought that when she'd had her face clean of makeup and her hair was tied in a scarf She didn't need Merchand products—not a one of them. Yes, she did! Every woman did. If he started thinking anyone didn't, he might as well go out of business in the cosmetic field, and he had made such a good beginning. She had made such a good beginning. *They* had.

But he didn't want anyone to see a picture of her in that revealing gown. "Put her in pajamas," he said. "Call me when she's ready "

Florence was back in thirty minutes with frilly, feminine pajamas. When Pat put them on, she looked years younger.

"This is ridiculous. Mr. Merchand wanted someone who looked older. A teenager doesn't need night cream the way older women do."

"I know," Florence said, " and the nightgown was designed especially for you and the product." She flopped into a chair. "He's lost his mind."

"No. He's angry with me. But I'm afraid he's cutting off his nose to spite his face. Get him back to approve me, then I'll put on the nightgown and go to the session."

"He'll fire us all," Thaddeus warned.

"You can leave, Thad. You can meet me in the studio for touch-ups. And, Florence, you can leave the minute I'm approved in the pajamas. No one but me will be to blame for my wearing the gown."

"I want to have the proper outfit worn," Florence said. "So you can't take all the responsibility. If you can face him, I can too."

"You needn't."

"I will."

"I might as well stay too," Thad said. "If we're all involved, his anger will be spread out and none of us will have to take the full force of it."

"All right," Pat said, but she knew if a hundred people were involved, it would be she that he would land on; she'd had the idea to deceive him. Well, she had offered to quit, and he hadn't let her. He could fire her if he wanted. She felt a kernel of apprehension as she recalled his threat to blacklist her. But she couldn't let herself be photographed in the kiddy pajamas; that would make her, him, *and* the company look foolish.

When Derrick returned, he looked at her critically, then nodded. "Better," he said, and Thad and Florence exchanged glances. He came to Patricia and tugged the collars nearer each other, as if he wanted even her collarbone covered.

She was keenly aware of where his fingers brushed her skin, but she forced herself to be calm. "Will I pass now?"

"Yes. Thank you," he said to Florence as he left.

The minute he was out of sight, there was a flurry of activity and within five minutes Pat was back in the gown and Thad had touched up her hair. "I hope we all aren't shot at dawn," he said.

"I'll see if the photographer can slow the proofs awhile before showing them to Mr. Merchand."

"Good idea. Put off the execution as long as possible." He shook his head. "Derrick gets more antsy about the cosmetic line every week."

"That's because he and I have a personality conflict. He probably should have hired one of the other girls"—she sighed— "because we don't get along at all."

The next morning Merchand again showed up the moment Pat arrived. He was checking on her, making sure she came to work, proving he didn't trust her. "You don't need to bother coming here every day," she said. "I'll be at work on time."

"Yes, you will, Miss Dayton. And please don't presume to tell me how to do my job. If I choose to visit the dressing room, I'll visit the dressing room."

"Yes, sir," she said, and went to the basin so one of Thad's assistants could wash her hair. She refused to look at Derrick again.

When she was camera ready, he came back. Today they were to do foundation or rouge or eye makeup, Pat wasn't sure, but she had on a demure suit. It had a slash neckline with too short an opening to reach her cleavage. Merchand wrapped a light patterned scarf around her neck and tucked it into the slit. "There. That's better."

The clean lines of the suit were ruined. Behind him, Florence raised her eyes toward heaven for help. "Thank you for your meticulous attention," Pat said, and was rewarded with a threatening look.

The moment Merchand was gone, the scarf came off and she reported for the sitting. So far no proofs had gone to him. "Do you think there is any way you can hold off until the entire series is completed?" she asked. This was to be a rush job, finished in a week, or they'd never have a chance of keeping them from the boss.

"We can try."

"Good." She was convinced Derrick would continue to visit the dressing room and try to cover her from head to toe as if she were a nun, and she didn't know many nuns who spent a great deal of time or money on cosmetics or perfume.

The next day she was supposed to wear pants, but Merchand had changed his mind. He wanted her in a suit or a dress. "A full skirt," he said.

"He's lost every bit of taste he ever had," Florence complained after he'd gone. "I don't know what's got into him."

"He's angry with me for doing something he didn't like."

"Is that a reason to destroy his campaign?"

"No, but . . . but he's afraid because of me, the image of Merchand cosmetics might be cheapened."

"By you?" Florence chuckled. "You look as pure as Mary Poppins."

Pat shrugged. "He doesn't think so."

"Ah-hah!"

"I want nothing to do with the man; I just want to do my job."

"Maybe that's part of the trouble. Maybe he wants you to want to have something to do with him."

"That's doubtful. He has a poor opinion of me. But I don't intend to spend a lot of time worrying about it, and none at all in trying to rectify it." That was a lie. She spent half her spare time worrying about why Derrick had taken such a sudden dislike to her. She would have spent all her time worrying about it, but with her excitement in getting ready for her wedding, Becky required some attention.

"Suit youself," Florence said.

And she did. Pat put on the specially designed black satin pantsuit as soon as Merchand had approved a full skirt and puritanical top.

The stills were finished—all of them—before they were sent for Merchand's okay. Pat didn't go in on the day they were to be sent to him. She considered going somewhere where he'd never find her, but she'd have to get permission to go anywhere and then he'd know where she was. She couldn't even go for a walk. If he tried to get in touch with her today—and she was certain he would—and she wasn't in, he'd be more angry.

It hadn't turned nine o'clock before the phone rang. "I think you know why I'm calling," Russell said.

"Yes."

"Come now." He hung up.

She would have to go as she was, and it was a good thing she was dressed, because at this moment she wouldn't have been able to fasten a button. She wasn't surprised at her attack of nerves, she'd defied Derrick blatantly. But he'd been distorted in his thinking; she knew she wouldn't cheapen the Merchand Girl image. The two episodes with the man on the beach had been the only lapses she had ever had—that and misjudging Bart long ago. But she'd been a mere child then; she hadn't known anything about the world or about worldliness.

Lord. If Merchand ever found out about Bart, he'd be convinced beyond hope that she was decadent.

Mrs. Kelsoe pursed her lips and watched as Patricia went through the room. Russell shook his head, flinched in exaggeration as if avoiding a blow from a heavyweight, then pointed at the door.

Pat could go no farther. She had got as far as the outer office, but she couldn't take the final steps. Merchand *might* fire her. What would she do then? She had reduced her bills considerably, but some still remained. She wouldn't be able to work in this profession again if he followed through on his threat. And she had no doubt he could blacklist her. Maybe she could survive as a shopgirl, but she didn't want to have to try; she shouldn't be forced to try, as she hadn't done anything wrong. What she'd done had been in the best interest of the company, not just in disobedience to Derrick for the heck of it.

She was within reach of the knob and she stared at the panel. Oh, Lord, she hated to open that door.

Russell coughed pointedly and she looked toward him. "Now," he mouthed.

Nearly all her strength drained through her feet as she turned the knob. She inched the door open with molasses slowness, and when she went inside, she tried hard to be invisible. But Merchand was at his desk, and his gaze was on her the moment she passed the shelter of the door. He didn't speak, so she forced herself all the way inside, shut the door carefully and softly behind her, then turned to face him again. He was still staring at her. He picked up an eight-by-ten glossy and spun it in the air to fall askew on the stack below.

"You—" Pat cleared her throat. "You wanted to see me?"

He slammed the palms of his hands on the desk and levered to his feet. His gaze was hard and filled with anger, but he didn't say a word. For a full two minutes he seemed to control an urge to leap on her and rip her apart. Then carefully, as though he might break if he moved rapidly, he lowered himself into his chair, deliberately took his hands from the desk, and forced himself to lean back in his seat. But his look never left her face, and he still said nothing.

Had he been struck mute?

Pat hadn't moved; she was right where she had stopped when she came into the room. She couldn't take his silence any longer. "Those clothes you wanted me to wear were ridiculous," she said, so low it was nearly a whisper.

"These are the ads for the Christmas campaign." ·

"I know."

He was infintely patient. "We don't have time to redo them."

"I know that too."

"You sabotaged me." His eyes hadn't wavered.

"If that's what you think, go on and think it. I think·I kept you from looking silly." She was terrified her comments would make him madder—though she wasn't sure he could become more angry— and he had no real reason to be angry with her. If he would look at things calmly, he'd see that what she had done had been in the best interest of the corporation. She hadn't disobeyed the actual letter of the corporation contract: she'd done her job to represent them to the best of her ability. She wouldn't have if she had dressed the way he had wanted her to.

"You might just as well have asked them to wrap me in a—" She had started to say sheet, but she didn't want that kind of connotation added to the conversation; just once she'd like a meeting with Derrick where sex wasn't a dominant force. "In a shroud," she said.

"The clothes are unimportant. I did at one time select those you chose to wear. They'll do." He hadn't stopped staring at her. "You don't have your look in any of these photographs; your expression is different; you deliberately tried to make yourself look like any hundred other models. Why did you do it? Do you want out of your contract? Is the job so distasteful to you?"

"No." She hadn't known her look had changed noticeably, but she had refused to let herself drop into fantasy. "I didn't know my expression was different."

"Come here."

Pat didn't want to leave the false security of the door, but she did. When she reached the desk, he stood and stuck the sheaf of photographs in front of her. "Take a look."

She glanced at the top one. It looked okay to her—maybe not as misty. She went to a chair. None of the pictures was bad; each would tell the world how wonderful Merchand products were.

"Well?" he said.

She glanced at him. "They'll do."

"*Do?* I want them to more than just do."

"As far as you're concerned, will they do?"

"I guess they'll have to, won't they?"

"So they will *do?*"

"Yes, dammit, they'll do."

She approached the desk swiftly. "Then I don't think you have any complaints, Mr. Perfectionist." She slammed the pictures on his desk. "Is there anything else, *sir?*"

"Yes, *madam,* there is. I want your expression back. I told you that was why you got the job; so get it back. I don't know what you have to do, but get it. That's an order."

"And what if I can't?"

Derrick let his gaze drift from her face along the line of her neck to touch the swell of her breasts and move down to the curve of her hip. "I think I know how to make you get the look, dear little employee of mine, so if you can't manage by yourself, I'll have to help you out."

Her face flushed immediately as she vividly recalled each time he had touched her.

"See?" he said softly.

Pat turned her back to him.

"I don't even have to touch you, do I?"

She sped to the door and out.

"Did you get fired?" Russell called to her as she raced across the room.

"No. Unfortunately."

Chapter Thirteen

As a matter of routine when Patricia got home, she checked her answering machine. Russell was recorded saying she had a date this evening. As usual, no who and no why; just when. She wasn't going to put up with that. She had a right to know who would take her and where she was going. She phoned Russell.

"Mr. Merchand didn't tell me about the appointment until after you'd gone," he said. "I think he meant to tell you himself, but you left in such a hurry."

"Sure he did." She didn't believe that for a second. He liked to give her blind orders and have her obey them blindly.

"You're to go to a reception for the mayor. Mr. Spears will pick you up. Just a second." There was silence a moment as she was put on hold, then he came back. "Mr. Merchand buzzed. He said you're to wear anything you please as long as it's formal. Be as sexy as you want. Show as much as you like."

"What!"

"His words, not mine," Russell said swiftly. "I guess he's still mad at you for wearing what you wanted for the pictures, huh?"

"I wore what he requested while he was still sane," she said and slammed the receiver onto the hook.

Pat pulled out the most blatantly sensuous dress she owned; it was cut nearly to the waist in front and had no back at all. She'd never had the courage to wear it before. In fact, she never would have bought it if Bart hadn't insisted. But Pat thought the gown inappropriate and stuffed it into the wastebasket. In its place she chose a sheath with a mandarin collar and slits up both sides. But this dress was out of date. Other than that thing she'd just thrown away and the dress she had worn when she had gone dancing with Derrick, she had nothing to wear. The only things she owned—well, sort of owned—that would do were the Merchand Girl clothes. If Derrick wanted her to represent his company properly, she'd have to wear one of those. She phoned Florence to see if the dressing room would be open.

"I'll meet you, doll," Florence said.

Pat had just put on her makeup and slacks and shirt when Becky came in from work. "Hi. Do you know it's snowing?"

"In October? Well, that's just wonderful."

"It won't stick. What are you doing with your hair up?"

"I'm going out. Orders."

"In that?"

"No, I'm going to change at the office. I haven't a decent thing here."

"After my wedding, you'll have your maid of honor dress. It's in style."

"I'll bet it is."

"You've got to go for a fitting, Pat. The wedding is in two days."

"I haven't done that, have I? I'm sorry. I guess I've been so busy, I forgot."

"As long as you don't forget the rehearsal tomorrow at two and the wedding Sunday at four."

"I won't. And I'll go for a fitting in the morning." She groaned. "Oh, Lord, I have to ask permission."

"You'll get it," Becky said confidently. "Is Derrick going to take you tonight?"

"No."

"Are you sure? I'll bet he does come for you."

"I'm sure he won't."

He didn't. At the stroke of the clock Edward Spears rang the doorbell. He was a large, paunchy man with giant jowls and bags under his eyes. "Ready, Miss Dayton?" he asked, then glanced at her slacks. "It's formal."

"I know. I have to get a dress. We can stop on our way, can't we?"

"Do we have a choice? But we have to hurry, we're expected soon."

"Right." Pat waved to Becky and grabbed her coat. She'd have to borrow a wrap from wardrobe too. So much for winning the battle of the snag.

Florence was waiting. With a smile and a gleam in her eyes, she held out the evening gown Derrick had wanted altered for the perfume ad they'd just completed. The dress was gossamer pastel with folds and gathers that did the most for her shape. "Got the courage to wear it?" she asked.

Pat smiled and shrugged. "What can he do but kill me?"

"Want me to sew the panel across the front?"

"Again?" She laughed. "I think once was enough."

"Do you want the necklace?"

"Why not? I'm a Merchand product, after all."

"I thought you might." She pulled it from her pocket and looped it around Pat's neck. The stone hung an inch above the elegantly draped neckline.

"This isn't a real emerald, is it?"

"No. But don't get mugged anyway."

"I won't." Pat looked at herself in the three-way mirror. The stone looked real and glanced green to reflect the sheen of the gown. Pat thought she could have stepped out of an advertisement—and she had. "I need a wrap." Florence brought out the fur stole that had been used in the same ad. "I'll bring all this back when I come next time. Thanks, Florence."

When she found Spears, he was pacing and glancing at his watch. "Well," he said and scowled, then he looked at her again. "Well!" he repeated. "You sure were worth the wait."

"Thank you. Shall we go?"

The taxi filled with the scent of Merchand perfume, and she thought maybe she had overdone it; she certainly was broadcasting the product.

The moment they reached the door to the reception room, Derrick came to them. "Thank you, Spears," he said and took her arm.

She tried to draw away, but his grip tightened. "Be civil," he said. "This is business." He looked at her dress. "As I can see you already surmised. I have some people for you to meet." Derrick linked his arm around her waist as he guided her from one person to another, none of whom Patricia knew and none of whom she would remember. She was conscious only of his hand on her. She wished there were some way she could get through the rest of her contract without this personal contact. The gentle way he touched her made it difficult to remember he disliked her and didn't trust her.

Since they had gone to the park, Derrick hadn't said a single pleasant word to her. And she didn't know what had happened to change him. Pat had done nothing on the tour that would bring disgrace to the company. Number one: she'd been too busy. Number two: she'd spent every spare moment thinking of him. Now she wished she hadn't—he didn't deserve it.

"That's Oscar Fane," he said softly, leaning toward her. "One of the most powerful men on Wall Street."

Oscar was the smallest man she'd ever seen, but he was perfectly proportioned. He was slim, his hair was fog gray, and his clothes were—the only word to describe them was—*natty*. He held himself proudly erect, and though his face was thoroughly wrinkled, his eyes and body movements ceded nothing to age. The woman beside him dwarfed him and was one of the most handsome women Patricia had ever seen. She too was old, but that didn't make the slightest difference to her beauty. As Pat watched, the woman touched Oscar on his shoulder and made a comment to him.

Patricia glanced at Derrick. "His wife?"

"Yes. Theirs is one of the few successful marriages I know. They've been together over fifty-five years. That's the kind of marriage I'll have." He glanced at her apprehensively, then rushed her through the crowd to introduce her to the Fanes.

They were charming. Mrs. Fane would have made two Oscars, but it was evident that when she looked at him, she saw one of the largest men she knew.

Derrick left Pat with them while he went to fetch champagne, then they mingled again. He introduced her to no man under fifty years old—another way of telling her she wasn't to be trusted. He introduced her to young women, but that could have been because he had no option; they sought him out. Some of them openly flirted with him, some boldly asked when he was going to call again, and each touched him one way or another. Pat recognized a few of them: some by name, others from pictures she had seen.

"Isn't she lovely?" Derrick said, looking across the room.

Patricia felt an immediate stab of jealousy as she followed the direction of his gaze, and though she hated to admit it, the woman *was* lovely. She was pale and exquisite, with hair that was too fine a color to be called blond: it was a silver cloud. She was slim and willowy and almost too beautiful to be real.

With more eagerness than when he had approached anyone else, Derrick began to edge them past the people barriers. As Pat looked across the room again Bart VanStang stepped to the woman's side and took her arm as if he owned it. He murmured something and she smiled, nodded, and glanced up at him.

Pat halted abruptly.

Derrick glanced down at her. "What's wrong?"

Her hand went to her throat. "The crowd," she said, knowing the feeble excuse couldn't explain her petrified state. She hadn't seen Bart in over two years, and she would have been much happier if she had never seen him again.

"Don't you feel well?"

"I—I'm fine. Wait. No. May we leave?"

It was too late. Bart and the lovely vision were coming toward them. "Patrish! My God! You're as beautiful as ever." Bart took her hand and bent to kiss it as if he were a gallant. She knew better.

"Bart," she said weakly. He had changed little; if anything, he'd grown more handsome, and he still had that undercurrent of male dominance.

"I've seen your ads. You've done well for yourself, I must say." He reached to touch her cheek in a familiar, distinctly intimate way, then glanced at Merchand. "Is this your benefactor?" He smiled as if they shared a secret on how to satisfy women. "She's a delight, isn't she?"

Derrick looked at her. "Is she?"

"I want you to meet *my* protégée," he said brightly. "You two have a lot in common, Patrish, so wonderfully sweet, but she's a little more reasonable." He drew the beautiful woman forward. "This is Veronica Truxo. She's a painter—an artist. And I must say she's loaded with talent."

As Patricia touched fingers with Veronica, she felt a surge of sympathy, and she wanted to tell the woman who and what Bart really was. "Hello."

"Happy to meet you," Veronica said, then took Bart's arm in both her hands and leaned against him. Pat knew what point their relationship had reached: she was relying on his decisions totally—and blindly.

"Well, Patrish," Bart prompted and nodded at Derrick.

The absolutely last thing she wanted to do was introduce Bart to Derrick. She glanced at Merchand. He'd swept his coat aside and, as if he were in jeans, had slipped his hands into his hip pockets.

"Bartholomew VanStang, Derrick Merchand," she murmured almost inaudibly.

Derrick nodded curtly. "Mr. VanStang."

Bart chuckled and gave Pat a conspiratorial glance, obviously thinking she'd told Merchand about him. He took Veronica's arm. "Miss Truxo," he said to Derrick.

Derrick's attention focused on the woman and his hands came out of his pockets so he could take one of hers. "You're an artist, are you? Good luck on your work."

She gave him a dazzling smile. "Bart's helping me."

"I'm sure," Patricia said.

"Excuse us." Derrick grabbed Pat's arm and dragged her away from them. He didn't say a word as they went to the exit, got her wrap, and left. He had his car brought around, and when they were seated, he took off with a screech. They had gone a number of blocks before he said anything. "Who was that man?"

She didn't answer.

He drove furiously for a time, catching lights at the last show of yellow, honking his horn at any slight infraction by another driver, cutting cars off, being an antagonistic menace behind the wheel. Abruptly he eased off the accelerator and the car slowed. "You knew him, didn't you?"

Pat swallowed. "I did."

"How well?"

She looked out the window at the rows of buildings. If she thought Derrick had disliked her before, she was certain of it now. She swallowed again. She wanted to explain, tell him she'd been young and inexperienced, desperate for someone to recognize her as something other than another face among the mass of faces in the city.

Derrick drove slowly awhile, evidently too busy with his thoughts to make the instant and belligerent decisions he'd made during the first of the drive. Then he took off again as if they were being pursued. Near her apartment he pulled into a parking space, barely missing scraping his side against the bumper of the car behind. He left the car parked crookedly, came to hold her door, and slammed it stoutly behind her. He took her arm with as much feeling as he would hold a loaf of bread. At her door he said, "We begin television ads Monday." He touched a finger to his forehead in a semisalute. "Good night." He started toward the elevator.

"Mr. Merchand?"

He stopped at the sound of her voice.

"Tomorrow is the rehearsal for Becky's wedding, and the ceremony is Sunday at four."

He turned to look at her. "So?"

Sometimes he could be highly perverse! "So I'm asking permission to go."

"Well, of course you may go." He turned away again.

She went to have her dress fitted, and it was feminine and flattering: nearly as lovely as the things Florence designed. Becky had been right when she'd said it was up to date. Now Pat would have something elegant to wear that wasn't Merchand's.

At the rehearsal Becky wanted to know what was wrong with her.

"I don't know, Beck. I'm just tired, I guess. I'm sorry." She forced a smile. "I'm so happy for you. For you and Morris." Her smile vanished. "I guess I'm envious."

"Don't be. Someday—"

"Stop." Pat made her smile come back. "There's no reason for you to be concerned about me. Look at me. I got my break, I've got a great career, I'm going to the top. Nothing can stop me now."

Becky grinned. "And who knows? Someday—and probably soon—you'll meet someone you can't live without. And he'll feel the same about you. The next wedding will be yours."

"No, it won't. I have a contract, remember?"

"True. But like you said: if he loves you, he'll wait."

There was the catch. If. If he loved her. But the only person she wanted to love her couldn't bear her.

The next day at the church Pat and Mrs. Cloud helped Becky into her lacy formal wedding gown. She looked like a figure off a cake, and her eyes looked as if they held some of the rhinestones that decorated her dress.

Pat led the procession down the aisle, walking slowly with the music. After she reached the altar, moved to the left, and turned to watch the bride enter, she saw Derrick at the end of a pew about halfway back in the church. She nearly dropped her flowers; she had no idea he'd be there. Had Becky invited him? Or had he come to check to be sure she hadn't lied to him about where she'd be? He had said he would watch her—and he *was* watching her; had been since the moment she turned. Pat glanced away. If the reason he'd come was to make her feel self-conscious and nervous, he had succeeded.

Leaning gracefully on her father's arm, Becky came down the aisle. When she reached the rail and took Morris's hand, Pat glanced at Merchand again. He was still watching her. He nodded—a bare tip of his chin. Was the signal in recognition? Or was he telling her to pay attention to what she was supposed to be doing? she wondered.

During the ceremony flashes of herself in Becky's place and Derrick in Morris's ticked her mind. Pat didn't want those thoughts. She wanted nothing to do with Merchand except what was absolutely necessary for fulfilling her contract. But that was almost everything. She couldn't visit Fanstasyland without him knowing about it. She couldn't even refuse to fantasize without him knowing about it.

Merchand was at the reception, but he made no move to join Pat. Becky *must* have invited him. Pat wanted to ask, but she never got the opportunity because the bride was constantly besieged by well-wishers and men who wanted to kiss her. Merchand was one of them. Pat turned away when she saw his head bend. She wanted him to kiss her and only her. She was being more foolish than she'd ever hoped to be. This was more impossible than her fantasy.

Pat went to talk to Becky's parents. "My baby is a married woman now," Mrs. Cloud said.

"Your baby just cost me a ruddy fortune," Mr. Cloud said, not at all romantic or sentimental. But there were traces of tears in his eyes.

Pat helped Becky change into her traveling suit, and just before she and Morris left, she threw her bouquet over her shoulder directly into Patricia's arms.

"I doubt it," Merchand said from behind her.

She turned to him and missed Becky's smile and satisfied nod. "What?" she said.

"The penultimate clause. I don't think the bouquet will carry enough luck to overcome that. Do you?"

She shoved the flowers at him. "I don't ever want to get married."

She went to tell Mr. and Mrs. Cloud good-bye; there

was no more need for her to stay, and she didn't have permission to go anywhere else. When she saw the best man leaving, she called out to him, hurrying to catch up. "Freddy, give me a ride, will you?"

"She doesn't need one," Derrick said. Pat whirled to look at him. "I think you forgot something." He held the bouquet toward her.

"I don't want them. Wait, Freddy! I do need a ride." Merchand shook his head. "No, Freddy. She has a ride."

Freddy grinned at the dictatorial tone and sauntered on.

"What if I don't want to ride with you, Mr. Merchand?"

He shrugged. "I can't very well let you go off with Freddy, now, can I? Who knows where you'd go."

"Home. That's all. I was going home."

"Then I guess you need a ride."

She glared at him. "I'll find one." She headed back the way she had come.

But Derrick clutched her arm. "This way."

She jerked free. "I told you—"

"And I told you you're cute when you're mad, but you've already showed me that, so you can stop now." He took her arm again and propelled her toward his car.

"You don't own me."

"Who does?"

"No one," she flared.

"That's good to know. But I do own your work for the next couple of years, so we might try being civil with each other."

"Civil!" she said, confident he hadn't the vaguest idea of the definition of the word.

"I can be if you can be. That's why I offered you a ride home."

"You *offered?* I'd hate to see you demand something."

"Would you?" His gaze caught hers, and she had to look away. She clearly knew what he was thinking.

The drive home was more sedate than the previous time, but just as silent. When Derrick stopped in front of her building, he said, "Do you want me to walk you to your door?"

"What's wrong? Afraid I'll bolt the moment I'm out of your sight?"

"Not at all." His hands draped dejectedly on the far side of the steering wheel. "Patricia, we're tied together whether or not we like it."

Her heart contracted. He objected to the legal agreement that kept them seeing each other; he felt trapped and he thought he'd made a mistake. He was as unhappy with the contract as she. But his unhappiness came because he hated her; hers, because she loved him.

He leaned across her and opened the door. "You'd better go up alone."

"All right."

"You don't have a roommate anymore, and if I come with you, I won't leave." He paused. "Neither of us wants that to happen, do we?"

"I guess not." But Pat wasn't sure what she wanted to happen or not happen. He was the most confusing man she'd ever met.

"See you at work tomorrow, Patricia," he said as she got out.

"I'll be on time."

"I know. And I won't destroy the costumes this time."

His car stayed until she went inside the building. In her room, Pat went to the window and saw him driving away.

Chapter Fourteen

Derrick looked into the dressing room moments after Pat arrived. He didn't say anything, and she knew he was still checking on her, but she didn't care; she got to see him.

Because the weather was chilly most of the time, all but one of the commercials were scheduled to be done in studio. As Patricia was being shampooed and made up she was given the short script. She was to be getting ready for a party—whether it was one she was giving or one she was to attend hadn't been specified, only that she was delighted with the prospect and doubtless expected to find her perfect mate. An anticipatory atmosphere was to prevail. She was to be in her seasonally decorated home and stop at the mirror in the entry to check her makeup. As if to herself, she would mention the positive qualities of her cosmetics, then she was to look dreamily at the camera and say, "Merchand," as if that were the answer to everything.

Before they did the first take, Derrick came and sat near the back of the room. Patricia was sure he'd settled in for the day. He made her nervous, but she refused to let it show as she went through the moves and the lines with professional expertise. Thaddeus came to lift and perfect one lock of hair. They tried again, and the flow of the gown wasn't right. Then again: one of her moves was awkward. She fumbled a line. The logo on the lipstick wasn't facing the camera.

Shooting was no different from any other time, but she was keenly aware of each take and each mistake because Derrick was in the room.

They took a break for lunch, and he strolled to be beside her. "You're not giving us that look of yours."

Her look had never been easy to get when she was doing television, and since she'd stopped fantasizing, it hadn't even appeared in stills. She didn't know what to do. "I'm trying."

"Maybe you're working too hard at it. Just let it come as you used to."

"You make me nervous."

"I'm not sure whether that's a flattering remark, but I want your look back. Go on and dream. Okay?"

Pat wondered what he'd say if she told him he was the only person she could dream about any longer; the only person she wanted to dream about.

"Give it to me or I'll take it from you," he said, and the look came on her face at his words. "What are you thinking, Patricia?"

She had no intention of telling him she'd thought of him holding her, kissing her, making love to her. "Nothing."

"Right," he said disbelievingly. "I'll be back after lunch."

Pat hoped he wouldn't return; without him around, she might be able to resurrect her fantasy lover. She wanted to do her best.

They were well into new takes before Derrick returned, but she had done no better. She had fixed her mind on her dream lover and he'd changed almost instantly into the man on the beach. The thought of the fisherman distorted her expression to the point that even the key grip wondered what was wrong with her. She couldn't dream, and the inability worried her as much as not being able to stop had a few months ago.

Once more they began. She came down the stairs, passed the Christmas tree, glanced at it with approval, then stopped at the mirror to be sure her makeup was all right. She said the words properly, pulled out a tube, and touched her lips with color while holding the logo so it was easily readable by the camera, which did an extreme close-up of it and the curve of her lip. Another glance into the mirror to see if her lips would pass inspection, a light smile as she saw they would, then a look toward the lens to say the final word. Derrick was just beyond the camera, watching her with an expression he'd never worn. If she hadn't known better, she'd have thought it was affection. "Merchand," she said.

Except for the gentle sound of the camera, total quiet was in the room. The director said, "God!"

Patricia snapped back to reality. She glanced at the director, who was smiling widely. "Beautiful, Pat," he said. "Perfect. We'll never improve on that look or the delivery. You were unbelievable. Every woman in America will have to have Merchand lip color."

"Thank you."

"We have to do the first of it again, though. Get more of the look earlier."

"All right." Now she knew how to give the camera what it wanted, and she didn't have to fantasize; she simply had to think about her boss. But thoughts of him were more hopeless than any dream she'd ever had.

Pat looked for him, but he was gone. She felt hollow wondering where he'd gone and what he'd thought about the absolutely infatuated way she'd looked at him and said his name. Why had she let herself fall in love with him?

As far as her look was concerned, the shooting went smoothly for the rest of the series. She couldn't have stopped thinking of Derrick if she had wanted to. The only ad that had taken more than one day was the location scene, for which they drove to a ski slope where she stood in skis to extol the virtues of Merchand moisture cream. But the wind was wrong, the light was wrong, the snow was falling too heavily; the background crowd was too sparse, too busy, too congested. They finally finished the ad, but Patricia thought that before they did, she'd catch pneumonia.

Derrick didn't return to check on Patricia in the mornings or to see how the shooting was going. Her look had shaken him. But when the series was wrapped up earlier than had been anticipated, he called her to his office.

"I want to thank you," he said.

"For?"

"Your work." He wanted to say for giving him the look he always wanted her to have. But a discussion about that had got him in trouble with her once before.

Derrick strolled to the window. His desire for her hadn't diminished. The first time he had seen her—on the beach before he knew who she was—he had felt the animal urge. Then he had met her and his desire hadn't changed; her look had made sure of that. Sometimes he had been unable to control his feelings for her, and he had handled her wrong. He had always handled her wrong, especially after the second time on Otter Key. She had been eager for that man, had wanted him, but to her the man hadn't been Derrick. He had been so tremendously jealous of himself, he hadn't been able to behave in a sensible way. Fortunately, Pat had defied him about his childish changes in her costuming. She'd lost the look, though, but when he'd asked for it, she'd given it back—maybe because she was afraid he'd force her to look that way. He had threatened to. No, he had never handled her properly.

Her reflection was hazed behind his in the window. "Would you be offended if I asked you to make a few appearances?"

"What? I don't understand. That's part of my job."

He faced her. "With me."

"Oh."

Derrick tried to smile. "Look, dammit, I know we don't get along, but we can't let you stay closeted all the time. The Merchand Girl should make more public appearances; generate more interest."

"I see," she said coolly.

"Is there anyone you'd rather be with? That young man from the university? We could outfit him and pay the expenses so you could be seen in the proper places."

Pat shook her head. "No. I don't think he'd go for it. And besides, his hair is too long."

"The fellow from back home?"

"What fellow from back home?"

"The one you phoned to ask to go out with."

"Oh. He's a family friend. He was here for a convention. I don't even know where he is."

"Who, then?"

"But I thought you said *you* were going to."

The woman was the most profoundly irritating person he'd ever met. "I said if you'd not object."

"Did I?"

He went to his desk as if he had remembered an emergency he had to attend. "I'll pick you up at eight, Miss Dayton. Take the clothes Florence designed for you. You'll be going out almost nightly, and we don't want the hassle of stopping here."

It was difficult for Patricia to keep the look of joy off her face. She'd see Derrick. Even if he was only doing his duty and she'd more or less forced him by rejecting anyone else he mentioned, she'd see him. She didn't know how she got to Florence's office—she must have floated.

Not only did Florence send the gowns and dresses and tops and pants, she sent underthings and nightwear. The clothes arrived in plenty of time for Pat to make a choice, but it was nearly evening before she became calm enough to decide. All the outfits were flattering, but the blue dress she'd worn in a mascara ad had always been her favorite. By eight, she was ready and breathless with anticipation. But the bell didn't ring. By five after she was pacing, thinking Derrick had changed his mind and would call and cancel or would send someone—anyone—else. It was fifteen after before the doorbell rang.

"Traffic," he said in explanation for his tardiness.

"I understand." She would have forgiven him for any excuse. "Will I do?"

"You?" He smiled at her. "You'll do."

Nearly every night for a month they were seen in the most public places: restaurants, Broadway openings, nighclubs, gallery shows, the Met. And each night Derrick went to her door with her, told her he'd see her the next time, then said good night. He didn't kiss her. He was afraid to. All he could think was that she lived alone, Becky wouldn't come dashing in, and she was lovely.

His work habits had been blown to hell. His compulsion to succeed had usually kept him at his desk late into each night, but now he delegated, and everything ran more smoothly than before. The improvement was due to a number of reasons; that he'd been spreading himself too thin was the major one. This was probably how he should have run the business from the beginning.

But each time Derrick thought of delegating the job of escorting the Merchand Girl, he rejected the idea, giving himself one reason or another. None of the reasons was true. He wanted to see her, to make sure she didn't have a recurrence of an episode like the one with him on the beach—unless she knew who he was.

It was December; the new campaign had been launched and sales in cosmetics were up with a stronger percentage than before. He had to give Patricia some time off; she deserved a break, and she needed one because the new year was going to begin with a difficult schedule. The line was to launch in Europe, and Pat would have to go there to make appearances and to film commercials in every capital city. Tonight was to be the last time he'd see her until after her vacation; she didn't even know he was going to let her go away. He planned an evening in a less populated spot, and instead of asking for the most public table, he requested an isolated one.

Patricia was puzzled when he took her to the secluded table in the out-of-the-way restaurant, but when Derrick began to lay out plans, she knew the privacy was only so they could talk business. She wanted to tell him she didn't want a vacation, didn't want to see her folks, only wanted to be with him. And when he told her about the tour in Europe, she couldn't look at him She wouldn't be near him for months. She had tried to think of ways to make him see her as a woman and not as a signboard, but she had failed. He hadn't even suggested kissing her good night. She nodded and agreed to everything he told her, but she felt wretched.

Before they got into the elevator, Pat made up her mind he wasn't going to leave her tonight with a simple good-bye—even if she had to broach it herself.

At her door Derrick looked at her a moment, then said, "I guess it'll be a while before we see each other again."

"Yes."

He touched a finger to his brow, and she knew he was going to salute and leave as he had each evening since they'd begun their appearances. Pat reached out to him. "Wait."

"Patricia."

His arms came around her and his mouth met hers, and they were right where they had been months before; as if only a second had passed since their last kiss. She couldn't get enough of his touch, couldn't get close enough to him. She was being as he had accused wanton, easy, a passionate flame turned on instantly by sensual contact. He didn't know only he could strike the spark.

"I want you," he said against her hair. He found the opening in her top and slid his hand inside. "God, I want you."

What did it matter what he thought about her? She wanted him so badly, she could die. When he slid her bodice aside so his mouth could reach her breast, she forgot they were in the hallway and someone could come along, and she held him closer. "Derrick," she said, brought to life by his caress.

"You know me," he said against her. Suddenly, he drew away and pulled her dress to cover her—but his fingers shook as he did. "This is a—uh—a physical attraction."

"I know what it is."

For a moment he caressed her breasts, stirring them through the cloth, then he let go. His eyes were cloudy with desire. "I'll see you."

"Yes. All right." Pat ached with need for him, but he'd rejected her again. "After New Year's." She fumbled in her bag for her key, found it, and put it into the lock. "Good night." The door opened, but he made no move to leave. Pat went inside and looked at him through the opening.

"Good night," he said.

"Good night." It was nearly impossible for her to shut the door, but she did.

She went to take off her dress, wondering what else she could have done to let him know she was willing. He had been eager too. It had been impossible for him to disguise his response.

As she hung up her dress the phone rang, momentarily irritating her. But at this hour the call must be important, so she hurried to answer.

"Patricia?"

He couldn't have had time to get home. "Yes."

"This is Derrick."

"I know."

"I'm on the corner."

Just hearing his voice made her breath short. "I wondered. I knew you wouldn't have had time to go home."

"I want to come back."

"All right."

"You know why."

She was silent for one heartbeat. "Yes."

"You'll let me come?"

Two heartbeats. "I will."

He hung up without saying anything else. What else did he need to say?

Pat stood beside the phone, clad only in a pair of panty hose with a terry robe pulled half over her shoulder. If anything could make him go away, it was the way she looked just then. She ran into the bedroom, throwing her robe off and ripping at her hose, finally having to stop to take them off. The peignoir Derrick objected to so strongly when she was to wear it in the ad was donned, along with the matching slippers as his tap came on the door

"Ah!" she exclaimed, startled and terrified. She couldn't let him in. She ran the first half of the way, then slowed and went the second half at a normal pace

Derrick came inside and looked at her a moment before he held out his arms. He didn't come to her, she went to him, and his arms closed around her.

"This is where you should be in that gown," he said. "Not in a picture for everyone to see. You're too desirable."

"You hired me."

"I did." His mouth covered hers a moment, then he lifted her. "Where's the bedroom?"

Unable to speak, Pat pointed. He carried her in and put her on the bed. "I'm not doing this right," he said, but didn't slow his rush. He shook off his jacket and attempted her peignoir at the same time. "You make me crazy." He forgot his clothes and concentrated on hers, finally sliding the straps of her gown from her shoulders. "I'm not being at all subtle or seductive," he said. "Just hungry for you."

She was busy with the buttons of his shirt. "Do that," she whispered and touched his buckle.

His hands obeyed quickly, but he did only minimal unfastening before he was back at work on her gown, trying to get it off her. She had to raise her arms so he could slip it over her head.

"Lights," he said.

Pat didn't know what he meant. The lights weren't on; there was just a glow from the living room, a faint one, scarcely enough to see by. She hadn't thought he would be shy.

He was up and away from the bed, turning on the overhead. "I want to see you this time." He finished stripping off his clothes, then slid onto the bed. "Oh, God, you look as good as you feel." Derrick looked at her a minute, then reached beyond her to turn on the bedside lamp. "You're lovely." He knelt astride her and touched a breast with each hand as if to see them were all he needed. It wasn't. He bent to first one then the other to tease them with his tongue.

Her arm fished between them to feel the springiness of the hair on his chest, then go lower. As her hand closed around him, he groaned and took her mouth. "Woman," he said into it. "I like the way you taste." He slid down her body; his hands followed his mouth, caressing each breast when his mouth was through, sampling her.

She had to be content with letting her fingers learn the shape of his muscles beneath his skin, the thick luxuriance of his hair, the feel of his jaw.

Derrick knelt upright, still straddling her. "Let me," he said and glanced at her eyes for permission; then he moved her legs so he was inside them. He stroked her thighs. "Yes." He began the slow search back to her lips. "You'll let me this time, won't you? You won't refuse."

She guided him in answer.

"I love the light." He propped his hands on either side of her so he could watch her welcome his unqualified and absolute possession. When he was fully hers, he lowered. "You," he whispered, and she began the rhythm.

If she had thought she would die without him, she knew she'd die with him. Never had she felt such rushes of ecstasy. Never had she felt more like she was where she should be, with whom she should be, doing what she should be. She lost all inhibitions. Not once did she think of him as her boss or as a dream; he was her lover. The need that had built in them was the single motivation of their world.

When she reached the tingling high wire before falling into climax, she screamed and raked her nails across his back. And as her body shuddered into spasms of release, she held him closer and shouted his name.

Her response triggered him. His hands dug behind her, bruising her with the force of his grip. He reached his peak, hanging on to it as long as he could, then he let go with a moan of pleasure

Exhausted, covered with a sheen from their exertion, they lay joined, each trying to recover his own identity, breathing to calm.

He levered onto his elbow, looked at her, and kissed her gently. "You're a noisy little thing."

"Am I? I didn't know."

He chuckled. "You are. My eardrums will never be the same."

She smiled shyly at him. "Do you object?"

"Not at all. It's good to know what you enjoy." Derrick rolled away, kissing her as he went. She looked at him quizzically, not knowing if he would dress and heedlessly leave her, treat their union as if it had been nothing but the casual quenching of an urgent drive. She didn't feel casual. Certainly not.

"Where's the bathroom?" he asked.

Pat pointed and he was gone a second and came back with a towel. He handed it to her, then got on the bed with her again. He slid his arm beneath her and cuddled her head on his shoulder. "We fit together, don't we?" he said. He had never felt he fitted anywhere as well. To have her always would be right, and he should tie her to him more permanently than by just the contract with his company, but he stiffened. "I'm not the marrying kind," he blurted.

She hadn't asked him, but she couldn't deny the thought would have come if she'd let herself think about anything other than the feel of him against her At Becky's wedding she had thought about marrying him. "And I'm not the promiscuous kind."

He laughed—a short, humorless laugh—and she knew his mistrust of her had come back. She drew away from him. "I'm not!" But how could he think otherwise? The first real opportunity she had—the first time he asked—she went to bed with him. "It's just that you—I—it's different."

"What about Bart? What about that, that, that—" He almost couldn't say it. "—that man on Otter Key?"

"Someone *did* tell you about that," she said, remembering her suspicion that the man had been on the Key when Derrick tried to find her. "Nothing happened."

"Only because he had restraint." Derrick sat up too, and glared at her.

A slow flow of anger began at her toes and worked upward. "And how do you know so much about it? Why do you choose to believe something you heard at least thirdhand? If it bothered you, why didn't you ask me?"

"I didn't need to ask you. I can tell by looking at you what you do and don't do."

She jumped off the bed. "And I can tell a lot about looking at you." Pat stood regally and stared at him. "The way people behave doesn't matter, is that it? Only appearances count. You don't care how people feel, what they think, what they want. All you've ever wanted with me was to hop in the sack. Well, you've done it."

"Yes, I have." He stood on the opposite side of the bed. "I think it was a mistake."

"Get out of here," she screamed. "Get out! Oh, God, if I *never* see you again it will be too soon."

"We have a contract."

Pat was so angry, she shook all over. "Yes, we do. We do have that." She tilted her chin to a more haughty angle. "But I don't intend to mix business with, with—" She didn't want to finish the familiar phrase.

"Pleasure?" he said wryly.

"No!" she raged. She looked for something to throw at him, grabbed her alarm clock, and threw it as hard as she could, but it snapped ineffectively—caught by the electric cord— and fell impotently on the bed.

"It was pleasure for me, dammit," Derrick shot at her. "But it was a mistake. I should never have touched you, but I'm not going to apologize. You wanted it as much as I did."

"Get out!" she shouted again. She drew herself up as tall as she could and pointed dramatically at the door. "Get *out*!"

"May I dress first?"

She bent and grabbed a handful of his clothes and flung them at him. They fell in disarray across the bed. "Yes! Dress!" She bent for more and tossed them toward him. One of his shoes had got kicked under the bed and she had to squat to get it out, and when she stood, she threw it at him. It sailed past his head and hit the wall with a crash.

"Thanks," he said.

She wasn't sure she could keep from crying before he was out of her sight. She had never hurt so badly. He thought she was cheap, and he'd taken advantage of it. Pat didn't want to cry in front of him; she didn't want him to see her so emotionally exposed. So she got up, marched into the bathroom, and slammed the door behind her.

After she heard him leave, she went back into the bedroom and saw he'd left his socks behind. She hoped his ankles froze. She picked them up and started to throw them in the wastebasket but changed her mind. Before her anger cooled, she wrapped them and addressed the package to his office. "Merry Christmas!"

Pat was glad she was going away. She had never

wanted to be out of the city as badly as she did now. In her terry robe, with the belt cinched tightly—almost painfully—around her waist, she began to pack. She would leave first thing in the morning. He probably wouldn't phone because of any shred of kindness or because of work—and she didn't want to be there to know he hadn't.

Chapter Fifteen

By afternoon Patricia was in Bridgeport. She phoned her parents from the station to give them a few minutes' notice. They hadn't known she had time off and was coming to visit. When the cab stopped in front of her childhood home, she felt good because she'd helped save the house for her mom and dad. After paying the driver, she carried her suitcases up the brick walk, which in spring was lined with daffodils and tulips, but now she crossed crisp dried curls of dead grass.

The door opened before she reached the porch, and her mother came out, looking too thin and pale, and much older than she'd ever looked in these familiar surroundings. She had been more wasted in the hospital, but no one expected anyone to be particularly robust there. "Mom," she said, dropping her bags and opening her arms.

"Patty."

As they clasped each other, tears came to Patricia's eyes because her mother felt even more fragile than she looked. "We'd better get you in the house. It's too cold for you to be out without a coat."

"Now, don't you start, Patty Dayton. Parnell is enough of a mother hen for me to cope with. I don't need two of you." She smiled at her daughter. "Why didn't you let us know you were coming?"

"Until last night, I didn't know I had any time off." She got her bags and herded her mother indoors, wondering what her parents would say if she told them why she'd forgotten to phone last night. She had been so angry and hurt and unsettled, she hadn't had a thought on her mind except to get out of the city and away from any reminder of Derrick. "Where's Dad?"

"He's still at work." He was manager for a men's store. "But if he'd known you were coming, he would have arranged his schedule so he could be here to greet you."

"Before Christmas when he's so busy, maybe it's a good thing he didn't know." Pat went up the stairs to her old bedroom, where she always stayed when she visited home.

The chintz spread and curtains were pleasantly familiar; she had selected the print years ago. The furniture was still the same. This was a warm and comfortable place to be—healing. She needed that.

When Pat unfastened her suitcase, she saw the package she had stuffed in the night before. She sat on the edge of her bed and looked at it. Again she started to throw it away, then decided to go ahead and put stamps on it and mail it. Serve Derrick right to be forced to remember the fiasco, to be shown he wasn't perfect— he couldn't even remember all his clothes. She hoped he'd think it was a gift, then when he opened it, he'd see it was nothing but his dirty socks.

Before her revived anger at him eased, she borrowed her mother's car and drove to the post office. They were locking the doors and she slipped inside the last open one. She sent the socks parcel post. That would show him she didn't want anything of his around. If she had thrown them away, he might have thought she was keeping them as a talisman. But she needed nothing to remind her of him.

Her parents asked about her job and about her boss, and she said what had to be said and no more; they asked about Becky. Pat realized she hadn't phoned to say she'd be out of town.

A lot of hoopla resulted from her visit to her hometown; pictures and articles appeared in the papers—but she wasn't Patricia Dayton anymore, she was the Merchand Girl. She was asked to be on morning and noontime local TV shows to discuss Merchand; she went and was civil—unless they asked about the man. Then she said she knew little about him; she only worked for him, after all.

Friends had seen her advertisements and wanted to hear the truth about Merchand products and about Derrick. They'd seen notices and pictures of him with her in the New York papers and were curious about their relationship. With complete honesty she could say theirs was nothing but a business arrangement.

Christmas Day was miserable—partly because she couldn't stop wondering what Derrick did on Christmas. His folks were dead, and she wondered if he went out or stayed home. She hoped he had to spend the time alone, hoped no one would want to have anything to do with him. And even as she thought that, she knew it was a ridiculous notion. A million people would want him to join them for the day

When New Year's Eve came and she went with her parents and Lester Brand to a celebration at the Elks Club where her father had been a member for years, she couldn't help wondering what female Merchand

had honored with his arrogant presence. And when
Lester—good old Lester, who now worked for his
father, who owned the Ford franchise, and who had
dated her a few times when she was in high school—
wanted to kiss her at the stroke of twelve, she turned
her cheek to him and said she had a fever blister. Poor
Lester.

On the fourth of January she had to return to New
York because on the fifth she had to report for work.
She was sure there were to be no photographic sessions; she would most likely be advised of the schedule
for Europe and fitted to new clothes Florence had designed for the trip.

Nothing from the Merchand Corporation was on her
telephone tape. Becky had left an invitation to Christmas Eve dinner, which went on to say if she didn't hear
within two days, she'd know Pat was out of town.

Patricia called and told her about the proposed Euro-
pean tour.

In the morning as she got ready to report to Merchand, she took excruciating pains with her hair and
makeup, but she spent more time trying to get herself
psychologically ready to see her boss again. In no manner would she show she thought more of him than he
obviously thought of her.

Though Pat knew Derrick had been at work since
seven, and she didn't get to the building until ten, she
looked for him in the lobby. He wasn't there. He
wasn't in the elevator either. She was poised and appeared unconcerned, but inside she was a quaking mass
of jelly. And she made it to the dressing room without
seeing him.

Florence was waiting with a large assortment of new
outfits: most of them were formal, each of them was
gorgeous. "Some of them are décolleté," she said.

"Do you suppose Mr. Merchand will insist the bosoms be covered in burlap?"

"I sincerely doubt it. I think he learned his lesson."

"Thank God."

The day was consumed with trying on the gowns and noting them for minor adjustments. No word came from above. No one came to see if she had reported as commanded. At four thirty Russell brought her itinerary and plane ticket. Obviously Derrick didn't want to see her any more than she wanted to see him.

"Touring Europe," Russell said. "Lucky stiff."

"Yeah. Lucky. Thanks, Russell."

The ticket was for a nine o'clock in the morning flight to Paris. "Lord," Patricia said. "Paris in January. What a thought."

"You fret?" Florence said. "All you have to do is catch a plane. I have to see to all the alterations on this stuff." She raked her hand along the line of hangers, making the dresses sway in waves of color. "He does give plenty of advance notice, doesn't he?" She shook her head as if she'd never get her work done on time.

Pat knew better. She could meet her deadline blindfolded and with one hand tied behind her back. "Am I supposed to take all the clothes?"

"No. Take some of the others you have; these will be shipped later. When they're done."

"They're lovely, Florence."

"You'd better believe it. I'd get canned if they weren't."

"I don't think you have to worry about that."

She grinned. "I don't. As long as there's a Merchand Girl, I have a job. Derrick looked as hard for a designer as he did for his first model. And even after you go, there'll be other Merchand Girls."

"I know." And Pat knew she'd never been anything to Derrick except a limited-run engagement. "I'm going to miss you while I'm in Europe, Florence."

"I don't think you'll have time." She glanced at the itinerary. "You'll be pretty busy. These clothes weren't made to hang in a closet."

"But you won't be there every day to dress me."

"I'll be *here* every day, working on things for the fall campaign. I envy you your trip."

"I'm looking forward to it." She didn't say the main reason was because for over two months she wouldn't be faced with the fear she could run into her boss. If she had that long, maybe she could work him out of her system and her mind. "What about Thaddeus?" she asked. "Where is he?"

"He'll be here when you come back. He's in California now, doing makeup for some movie or another Don't worry, they have cosmetologists over there if you find you need one "

"I wasn't thinking about that. It just seems odd not having him here. He's usually here."

"He'll be back when you are."

Pat was selective about the clothes she packed. With the new ones coming, she wouldn't need many of the old ones. When she loaded her cosmetic case, Merchand's name looked at her from every tube and jar and bottle. But at least the man would be out of her sight for a while. If all she had to see was his name, she could live with that.

She went to Kennedy Airport early and had to wait for her flight to be called. She had a first class window seat, and though she wouldn't be able to see much except clouds and the Atlantic far below, she was glad to have the view. It would be evening in Paris before she got there, but she'd feel it was teatime. She pulled out her itinerary to see what she had scheduled for tomorrow; she knew she wouldn't be able to sleep properly tonight, that she probably wouldn't drift off until early morning, and that she'd be haggard tomorrow if she had to get up at a normal time. She had a free day: someone had thought about jetlag.

Pat began to flip through the pages to see where the tour would take her and someone sat beside her. She shifted her arm out of the way, still looking at her routings. The man tugged at his seat belt, which was jammed between him and the armrest, and swore gently. The last time she had heard that voice was in her apartment through a closed door, saying the same thing.

Ignoring her appalled stare, Derrick got the belt out and put it on, then opened a magazine.

"What are you doing here?" she asked, valiantly trying to keep her voice controlled and civilized.

Derrick glanced at her. "You didn't think you were going to be allowed to go bopping all over Europe alone, did you?"

She hadn't thought about it at all. She had been told what to do for months, and she had assumed she would be told what to do when she landed in Paris. "But—"

"No buts. This is my company, this is my campaign, and I have to go." He pointedly began to read, through with the conversation.

"You could have got another seat."

He raised his eyebrows and looked at her again. "Why?"

"Because." That was a most illogical answer. Childish. It said nothing and said everything.

"We work together and we have to see each other, why put it off?"

"Because," she said again.

"If one day will make any difference, I'll be glad to move."

Patricia quit looking at him. She thought she would be away from him for months, and here he was close enough for her to touch. She shifted, afraid she might do just that. One day wouldn't make any difference, she hadn't been altogether sure months would. "Don't bother," she said.

"If you say so." He went back to his magazine.

She wasn't conscious of the plane taxiing because she was too completely aware of the man next to her. The first external sensation she had was of the thrust and lift of the jet into the sky. Instinctively she gripped both seat arms, and her elbow brushed his. She jerked away and leaned to look out the window at the receding city; then there was nothing but the sea with long white frills on it, and here and there the dot of a boat.

A flight attendant came to offer coffee or a drink. Patricia thought perhaps a Bloody Mary wouldn't be a bad idea; the calming effect of a drink might make sitting beside Derrick easier on her. But she asked for coffee. She would have to be totally drunk to forget he was there.

He asked for coffee too, and the attendant efficiently snapped down the trays and passed cups to them.

Pat sipped and looked out the window at more dashes of white, more dots of boats. Every so often she heard Derrick turn a page. She should have brought a book; she'd have had plenty of time to read one. She had nothing to do. She should have asked for a magazine. Dashes and dots. And she needed to go to the bathroom. She glanced at Derrick, seated so complacently beside her, and knew if she got up to go, she'd have to brush his legs or ask him to stand.

She'd wait.

Five more hours? All the way to France? she thought.

"Excuse me," she said, unbuckling her seat belt.

He glanced at her. "Running away?"

"No. If you must know, I have to relieve myself."

"Great Scott," he said.

She scooted forward in her seat. "Well?"

"You didn't say you had to go to the little girls' room or the ladies' room or even the powder room."

"So?"

"In this world full of euphemisms, you said you had to relieve yourself."

"I do. So if you'll please let me out...."

A smile tickled his lips and he turned his legs to the side to let her pass.

She went to the diagonal door and it was locked: someone had beat her to it. She had to wait. She glanced at Derrick, who was watching her—and continued to do so until she got her turn. Once inside, she thought it might not be a bad idea to stay there for the entire trip. Someone knocked.

On her way back to her seat Pat got a magazine. It wasn't one she particularly liked, but she had grabbed without looking. A picture of her was in it. A blue sleeve showed beside her, and she thought the picture must be cropped from one taken at her introduction when Derrick was in his tuxedo. She learned more about music stars, movie stars, model stars, and merchandizing stars then she'd ever hoped to know.

And it was only lunchtime. The attendants brought a

prepackaged, microwaved offering, and as Derrick made room for a tray to be passed to her, he bumped her arm and she flinched. She heard his hiss of impatiently expelled air. She wouldn't look at him, merely ate silently and listened to the murmur of happier passengers carrying on sotto voce conversations with their seat mates. Plane passengers and people waiting in hospital corridors spoke with the same low-keyed delivery

When they had eaten and the trays had been removed to be replaced by another round of coffee, Derrick pulled out one of his slim cigars. "Mind?" he said

Pat glanced at him and it, across the aisle at a man who already had one of the things going, at two people who were smoking cigarettes. "I see you made sure we'd be in the smoking section," she said. "I don't smoke."

"I do. And you're with me. Do you mind?"

"What difference does it make? The air is already so full of fumes, you can't breathe."

Sparks of anger danced in his eyes. He rolled the end of the cigar in his mouth a couple of turns, then languidly lit it, sucked on it, and let the smoke drift away He said, "Too bad you have only one vice."

Pat flushed. She was going to avoid mention of their last meeting, forget it, and he could have had the decency to do the same. She turned to look out the window again. Clouds were below, obscuring the dots and dashes, then letting them be seen. A few larger dark unidentifiable things were in the ocean too. The view was just as boring as before, but she was more determined not to look at her boss.

Eventually, she heard him stub out his cigar and get up. She turned from the window and discovered she'd got a crick in her neck from keeping it in the same position for so long. Merchand was on his way to the euphemism. She wondered what he called it. There were dozens of ways to say it; as many words for that as the Eskimos had for snow.

While he was gone she'd be free to get another magazine without asking him to move and without touching him. She bolted from her seat and grabbed one, without looking again, and was back in her seat before he came out. She wasn't wild about this magazine either, and there was a picture of Merchand in it.

He came back and before he sat asked, "Need to go again? It'll take us awhile to get out of the terminal after we're down. Customs, you know."

She decided she'd better. When she returned, she had to slip past him. He laid his legs toward her seat, and when she sat, her skirt draped over his knee. Before he swiveled straight again, she felt the warmth of him through the cloth and the memory of how incredibly warm his skin could be crashed into her mind. She put her forehead against the windowpane, hoping it would have some coolness to transmit to her. It didn't.

Never before in her life had she been so uncomfortable. She hated Derrick and she loved him; she didn't want to be so near him, but she didn't want to be anywhere else. She wished he hadn't said their making love was a mistake.

The pilot was telling them when they'd set down at Orly, what time it was there, and what the weather was like. Then they were down and taxiing toward a stop. The sounds of talk grew more animated, and rustles began—much too soon—of people pulling out their carryons. She did too. She got her cosmetic case, which held Merchand's name so many times. Derrick got into his jacket and squared his tie. When the flight attendants began to bring personal belongings, the wool coat was handed across to her, and he intercepted it.

"No," he said. He got up and took the coat with him to the storage closet, pulled out a plastic dress bag, removed a rust-colored coat from it, put the old one inside, and rehung the bag. He returned to the seat and without a word handed the new coat to her. It was cashmere and felt like down. She wasn't sure what to say to him, wasn't sure what the gesture meant; it brought too many memories.

He sat and looked at her "We never did do an ad with an ordinary coat, did we?" he asked softly.

She shook her head.

"I often give employees Christmas gifts. That's yours. No strings."

Pat glanced away from him, out the window again. He'd said the wrong thing. She wished they could begin all over, on equal footing somehow.

After the doors were opened, she picked up her overnight case, but he took it from her. His hand closed over hers on the handle, and an immediate awareness shot up her arm. Her gaze flew to meet his.

"Let me," he said. More was implied in those words than either was able to manage. "Carry the bag for you," he added. "Let me be a gentleman."

Pat relinquished her hold and the weight of the case tugged at him. He glanced at it and back at her. "What the devil do you have in here?"

"Cosmetics."

Derrick let a smile come slowly to his mouth. "You're stronger than you look. This is heavy."

"You don't package anything in plastic, it's all in glass or metal." She paused. "Except the tubes. I guess they're plastic."

"I guess they are." He stepped back to let her precede him, and she felt the light touch of his hand on her waist as they left the plane.

The taxi let them out on the Rue Cambon side of the Ritz Hotel, and when they went in, Derrick was greeted as if he were an old friend. He was. He stayed at the Ritz each time he was in Paris. He introduced Patricia to the manager, then they were led to a suite. When the porters took both sets of luggage inside, she balked.

"We have separate rooms," he assured her.

The porters grinned at each other at the remark and separated to carry her suitcases to the left, his to the right: they knew that in Paris the distance between doors was short.

As soon as the bellboys left, and without speaking to him, Patricia went to her room. Twice he went to her door to knock, but both times he stayed his hand; she'd have to come out sometime, get hungry or curious about their schedule.

He wandered to look out at the Place Vendôme. He'd never been in a similar situation in his life He wasn't going to touch Pat, he knew that, but he wasn't able to let go of her entirely. He had gone out with no one since he'd been with her; he hadn't wanted to be with another woman. Most of the time he had been able to concentrate on work, and he spent his time on it—constant time—through Christmas Day and New Year's Eve. But he'd fretted to know what she was doing.

The only bright spot during the holidays came when he got the package from her He wasn't sure precisely what message she wanted to convey by sending his forgotten socks, but she had wrapped them, addressed them, mailed them. She had thought about him.

He didn't have to be in Europe with her; he could have sent Murdock. Ryan would have known what to do more thoroughly than he did but, again, he hadn't been able to delegate where she was concerned. He went to her door and rapped sharply.

A minute later the door inched open and she looked at him. "Patricia," he said. He'd never squirmed before, never apologized before; he didn't know how. "Patricia," he repeated. She was still in the suit she'd worn on the plane; she looked sweet, and vastly suspicious of him. But she had wanted to make love as much as he had, she had been as eager as he. There was no reason to bring that night up, no need to make excuses. "Let's join the beau monde tonight," he said. "It's early to us, so we won't be able to sleep soon, and they stay up till all hours. Are you hungry?"

"I could eat."

He was relieved she wasn't going to be difficult. "Then put on something fancy. We'll do the town."

They went to Boulevard Saint-Germain to Les Deux Magots where, after discovering she spoke not a word of French, he ordered for the two of them: a light dinner of smoked salmon.

"I'll introduce you to gourmet cuisine tomorrow," he said. "After then I'm afraid our small vacation will be over. We'll have to get down to work." He smiled at her sitting in the wicker chair across from him. There was something compelling about the atmosphere in this city. Maybe it was only legend that Paris was the city of love, but he wished things could have been better between them. He took her hand off her wineglass, and she didn't try to pull away. He considered the possibility of changing his mind about how he'd decided to behave—the possibility of trying to change *her* mind.

They went to a boîte, and dancing with her was different but the same, worse but better, than when they'd danced together before. She seemed closer, warmer, more a person. But he was determined to keep things platonic between them. He made no move on her; he was a perfect gentleman. And she was a perfect lady

At two the true beau monde began to arrive: movie stars, artists, authors, singers—the beautiful people of the world. Not much later Derrick and Pat left to return to the hotel. During the ride she couldn't get enough of Paris at night. She twisted and turned in her seat, trying to see everything at once.

"I thought the Eiffel Tower would be lit," she said. "Or Notre Dame. They're famous tourist attractions."

"They aren't lit in winter; it isn't the tourist season. Are you disappointed?"

"A little."

He smiled at her little-girl exhilaration. "We'll fix it," he said.

For a split second, just before they parted in the sitting room, Derrick almost lost his resolve; he was going to kiss her good night. But he didn't. He said he'd see her in the morning and hurried to his room.

Derrick was gone when Patricia woke. A service with coffee was in the sitting room, and he'd left a note saying he'd soon return. She was bathed and dressed before he came back.

"I've made the arrangements, and we go to work tomorrow morning at the Louvre," he told her. "At least you will. I have business appointments. But today, for the rest of the day, we're tourists."

They went for a walk in the Luxembourg Gardens.

Lovers strolled hand in hand amid children rushing to ride the donkeys, to watch a puppet show, to sail boats in the pool. Occasionally the lovers stopped to kiss, and each time Pat saw an affectionate embrace she felt defeated. She went with Derrick to visit the Basilica of the Sacré-Coeur on the hill of Montmartre. They went to the right bank of the Seine and wandered along the Quai de la Mégisserie where, for three blocks, pet shops had their samples in cages on the sidewalk.

Derrick had been a gracious gentleman all day, concerned only with her introduction to the city, but as their dinner progressed he began to glance at his watch until Pat was certain he was getting bored with her company. At a minute before the hour he told her to look out the window. He pointed and she looked, and the Cathedral of Notre Dame blazed into light.

"Oh! How did that happen?"

He smiled, totally satisfied with himself. "Paris wants to please."

"But how did it happen? How did you know it would?"

"Things like that can be arranged. I didn't want you to miss seeing it."

"Thank you. It's lovely." Pat divided her time between looking at Notre Dame and looking at Derrick. He had said he would fix the darkened attraction, and he had. When they were served wild strawberries for dessert, she had to eat them by feeling for them with her fork; she couldn't take her gaze off the cathedral or the man who'd had the lights turned on.

He didn't let her dawdle until Notre Dame went dark; he rushed her to a cab and they rode to Parc du Champ de Mars. Once again overly concerned with his watch, he settled her on a bench facing the Eiffel Tower. As if at the wave of his hand, it, too, lit up. Pat gasped in delight, and he smiled.

"Another attempt from Paris to please you."

The city wasn't trying to please her, but Merchand was. She wasn't sure if she should be happy or sad about his effort. His light show could be an apology for taking advantage of her need for him, or it could be simply because he wanted her to be entertained. "How can you get them to turn on the lights?" she asked.

"They'll do it for anyone who pays ten percent over the cost of electricity plus the price of labor. We have it for an hour." He sat and put his arm on the bench behind her.

She wanted that arm touching her, wanted him to kiss her, hold her. "Derrick," she said.

"Yes?"

She couldn't ask for a kiss. "Thank you for the lights."

"Thank you for making me think of them." His hand touched her shoulder tentatively, then his arm slid around her. "Patricia?"

"Yes," she said, tempted to hold her breath as if that physical act would improve the chances of his filling all her wish.

"Tomorrow we have to go to work, but tonight is special."

"It is. You've made it so."

"*You* have," Derrick said and, to keep her from arguing the point, covered her mouth with his.

When he drew away, he saw other people had filtered into the park to take advantage of the sight, and he wished he hadn't had the lights turned on. He wished it until he saw again the joy on her face and the tower, reflected tiny and aglow, in her eyes. He smiled, glad again he'd planned the show, and sat content beside her, holding her comfortably. But he was shockingly aware of every move she made, no matter how slight. Even her breathing transmitted sensations, and the sensations were of more than life—they were of need and warmth and future. He knew he should move away from her, but he didn't, just held her until the lights on the tower went out.

After they returned to the hotel, Derrick went directly to his room and didn't behave for a minute as if he wanted to touch her; he'd been reserved on the taxi ride too. Pat couldn't understand—he'd been so warm in the park. She wished she had fantasy to escape into; she needed dreams worse than she ever had. But now he had a name.

Derrick was gone again in the morning, but this time he didn't return. Monsieur LeMoine, the coordinator for the photographic sessions in Paris, came to fetch her. She was whisked to a studio where she was groomed and dressed in one of the gowns Florence had sent; then she was taken to the Louvre.

Patricia was back at the hotel in time to dress for dinner with Derrick, but they didn't dine alone: LeMoine was with them, and Mademoiselle Tondu, the director of the French arm of Merchand, with her executive secretary, Monsieur Bonnetain. Most of the dinner conversation was in French, and though Pat knew they were discussing business because they looked at her often, she hadn't the slightest idea what facet of it they considered.

After Derrick took her back to the suite, he apologized for the language barrier and explained they had spoken French out of respect for time. He and she wouldn't be in France but a week longer, and plans had to be solidified quickly. Then he excused himself and left, and she wondered if he had other business meetings or if he were going to meet Mademoiselle Tondu for a more personal conversation. The woman was lovely, petite, and effervescent—and she had been visibly interested in more than the business angle of Merchand.

Patricia had never changed clothes so often, gone as many places, and understood as little as she did during that next week. Everyone knew some English, but the majority of the time French was spoken. She saw Derrick only at dinner. Each evening they were in a different elaborate restaurant, and each time they were joined by one or more associates.

When it was time to catch the train for Bonn, she was glad. The ride would provide a chance to relax.

"You have nerve," she said to Derrick, who was beside her on the bench seat in the train.

"How's that?" he asked.

"Trying to sell your perfume in France. American perfume yet. Such audacity!"

He smiled. "I can do it."

If Pat thought the Paris effort had been strenuous, she learned better: that had been nothing compared to the travel and schedule afterward. They left Germany and went to the Netherlands, they flew south to Italy and Egypt and Greece, then they went north to Spain

She saw Derrick every day: briefly here, briefly there. Dinner was the longest span of time she spent near him, but someone was always with them. She was a billboard to him and nothing more. But she thought about him constantly. She had to get proper expressions, and to do that she had to think of him. Even without that necessity Pat was sure she couldn't have stopped thinking of him. But none of her thoughts was optimistic, none of her dreams had a happy ending.

They were doing a commercial beside the monument to Miguel de Cervantes in the central Plaza de España in Madrid when she collapsed.

She came to with a cold cloth on her forehead. She was on her bed in her room, and Derrick was beside her, looking worried. They had shared quarters for the entire trip, but this was the first time he'd been in her room. "What happened?" she asked.

"Very original," Derrick said. "You tell me."

"I have no idea. I feel fine."

"Well, you didn't half an hour ago. You were green."

"I hope I went with the outfit." She tried to smile at him, but he was either too angry or too concerned to appreciate her humor.

"You didn't. But the outfit went with you—right down to the ground. You gave way completely." His expression was one of absolute distraction. "Do you do this often?"

"I've never passed out in my life."

"You've been working too hard. I've been pushing you too much."

Pat shrugged and didn't disagree, but she had worked hard before. "It could be the pace, I guess."

"We can cancel England, Scotland, and Ireland."

"I feel fine now. Really, I do."

"Are you sure?"

"Of course I'm sure," she said, thinking her collapse could have been caused by the desperate need she felt for him all the time. She saw too much of him, yet too little. That could make her sick—it did make her sick. Hopeless things always did. "I think maybe I just needed a nap."

He dipped a new cloth in a bowl of iced water sitting on the floor beside him, wrung it thoroughly, and placed it carefully where the other had been. "I've asked the hotel physician to come see you."

"Tell him not to come. I don't want some doctor telling me what's wrong with me in some language I can't understand. Anyway, there's nothing wrong with me. My blood pressure probably dropped suddenly. If I get any other symptoms, then when we get to Britain, I'll have a doctor. But not here."

"I could tell you what he said."

"I don't want a translation. I want to hear for myself. But nothing is wrong, I feel fine." She looked at Derrick sitting beside her bed so solicitously. He had been kind and considerate all during the trip, and it had been obvious he was determined nothing intimate would happen between them. "Derrick, please phone and tell the doctor not to come."

"You still look a little pale."

"I'm not pale. I'm fine." Pat threw back the cover and saw she was in only her underwear, and threw the cover back on again. "How did I get here?"

"I brought you." He got up. "I'll phone."

"But you weren't in the plaza," she said.

"I was there. I'm often around when you work. I was in the background." He went toward the door. "You haven't eaten today, have you?"

"No."

"I'll get you something."

As he went toward the phone in the sitting room, Derrick thought Pat was looking better, as if nothing had been wrong only a short time ago. Maybe she had heard from her parents before he had; maybe she was worried about her mother and that had caused her to faint. He wanted something other than his making her work too hard to have caused her collapse; he didn't like to think of himself as a Simon Legree who had driven her to illness. But the wire the porter had brought seconds after Derrick put her to bed had the feel of fresh news—and he wondered how he would tell her.

He ordered her some soup and canceled the doctor, then went back to her room. Pat looked even better. He fingered the cable he'd stuck into his hip pocket; he wouldn't have thought of mentioning her mother if she hadn't perked up so much. She looked almost normal again—maybe a bit fatigued.

But he wasn't telling her anything; he was just staring at her.

"Derrick," she said softly.

The sound wrenched at him. But he wasn't going to touch her: that was too dangerous, it made him think of permanence. "What?" he asked almost brusquely.

Her eyes took on an instant look of rejection. He wanted to grab her, hold her, tell her he loved her

"May I have a robe?" she said. "I'd like to sit up."

She *was* better. That had been rebellion he'd seen, not rejection. "Certainly." He went to her closet to fetch one, handed it to her, and turned his back so she could put it on. When he heard the sound of her sitting on the edge of the bed, he turned. "You got a cable."

Pat turned pale again, and he went immediately to her. "Your mother is all right. But she had to go back into the hospital."

"Oh, God."

He thought she might faint again. He shouldn't have told her, she hadn't known—and it was his pushing her that had caused her collapse.

"What did it say?"

"Just that she is in the hospital and everything is under control."

"That's Dad, he sent it; he didn't want me to worry. But he's worried. I have to call." She started to get up.

"Let me do it," he said. "When he's on the line, you can come talk."

"He may not be home; he might be at the hospital."

"I'll have them try both." But when he got the desk, he hit a snag. He went back to Patricia. "The lines are down. The phone company is working on them."

"How long will the repairs take?"

"They weren't sure. A couple of hours."

"I thought within minutes I'd be talking to Dad so I'd know what's wrong with Mother."

Derrick couldn't stand her look of worry. He went to her and put his arms around her, trying to offer comfort. This was the first time he had held her without thinking of her physically, but this time, comfort was his only motive. And she didn't fight him; she drew strength from him. He put his finger beneath her chin and tipped her face toward his. "Let's postpone the British part of the tour. We can. For a week, or longer if need be; we'll go home and see how she is. Okay?"

"Won't that put the schedule too far behind?"

"No. Forget the schedule. We don't have to do Britain if we don't want to. I can send someone to handle the business end of it, and we can get the pictures any time. Okay?"

Tears came to her eyes and one of them rolled down her cheek. "Yes. I'm so afraid it's cancer again. I'm not sure Mother can survive another operation; she was so weak when I saw her last."

"She'll be all right." He stood. "I'll see when we can get out of here."

It took him only a moment to learn from the in-hotel agent that a plane was due to leave almost immediately When he went back to her, she was dressed. "We can take off in an hour if we get to the airport on time."

"What about the phone call to Dad?"

"We'll be on our way before they get the lines fixed." He paused. "Would you rather wait?"

"I don't know what to do."

"Then, let's go. The next direct flight isn't until tomorrow." He picked up her suitcase, then hesitated. "Are you sure you're all right? Maybe you aren't well enough to travel; you were in bed not thirty minutes ago."

"I'd forgotten. I feel fine. I must have known—extrasensory perception or—" She started to cry and stopped herself. "I think I'd be worse if I stayed here."

"We need a break anyway. I was working you too hard."

As they went through the lobby he left instructions for their things to be packed and shipped to the London hotel. He also asked them to call his man and order his car and a weekend bag to be at Kennedy when they landed. "I'll drive you from there," he told Patricia. "You can't be sure you'll get good connections."

They were as silent with each other going back over the Atlantic as they had been on the first crossing, but this time Pat didn't flinch when Derrick touched her

After they were in the terminal, he nodded toward a phone. "Why don't you give your father a call while I start through customs?"

She smiled at him gratefully and went to try, but she had caught up with him before he'd got through. "No one answered," she said tensely.

"It's still visiting hours; maybe he's just visiting her."

"I know," she said, but he heard her doubt and fear.

"She'll be all right."

Edgar, Derrick's driver, was waiting when they went outside; the car was parked in front of the doors. Derrick thanked him, said he'd be home in a day or two, and told him to take a cab.

"How did he manage this?" Pat asked. "Anyone else would have had their car towed."

"Edgar has his ways. He's a good man."

"I can see that." She was trying to be light, easy. "Let there be transportation." But her concern came back and she looked at him, fogging up again. "Thank you, Derrick."

Chapter Sixteen

It was late night by the time they drove into Bridgeport—nearly dawn, already daytime in Madrid. Patricia
felt grainy with fatigue and lack of sleep. She glanced at
Derrick and knew he must be tired too, but he hadn't
made a single impatient comment. They'd stopped to
get coffee a couple of times, and she had phoned home
and still no one answered. They went directly to the
hospital. Pat was stiff from sitting and weak with worry
and her legs had begun to shake; she could scarcely
walk. She wouldn't have made it to the large glass
doors, much less through them, if Derrick hadn't held
her up and propelled her forward. When they got inside, the woman at the reception desk thought he had
brought her as a patient.

"No," Pat said. "I want to see Mrs. Parnell Dayton."

"Visiting hours don't begin until—"

"I'm her daughter. I just got into town. My father is
up there. She's Martha Dayton—Martha Bain Dayton."

"Oh," The receptionist gave the room number, and
they started toward the elevators. "Sir?" she said, trying to stop Derrick.

"I'm the son-in-law," he said over his shoulder and kept going.

He had said that only so Patricia wouldn't have to be alone. It was just an excuse. But his arm had gone more snugly around her as he said the words.

In the elevator Pat said, "Thank you. I didn't want to go alone."

"I know." He pulled her to him, tipped her chin upward, and brushed her lips with his. His hand roved from her waist to feel the swell of her breast. Even in this place with her as distracted as she was, he felt the stirring of desire. He had planned not to touch her, not even this much, not even in friendship, but she was so worried. He held her face and kissed her more solidly. "You'll be all right," he said.

The elevator doors eased open, and they went into the dimmed corridor. As they passed the nursing station one of the nurses tried to intercept them. "My wife wants to see her mother," Derrick said without slacking his pace.

Patricia looked at him. That was the second time he'd said they were married and it made her feel strange. It sounded so wonderfully right but was so undeniably out of the question.

He glanced at her and shrugged. "They wouldn't let me come otherwise."

The door to Martha's room was open, and they went in. Pat couldn't tell much about her mother; she was pale with an intravenous tube running from an inverted bottle to her arm and a nasogastric tube taped in place in her nostril. She was asleep. In a chair beside the bed, Parnell was nodding. "Dad?" Pat whispered.

His head jerked as if he were dreaming and her calling of his name had blended into the dream without disturbing him. "Dad," she said again, more loudly.

He woke and, bleary eyed, looked at her. "Patty! What are you doing here?" He got up and herded them into the hall so they could speak without waking Martha. "What are you doing here?" he repeated.

"What's wrong with Mother?"

"I told you I had everything under control. You didn't need to drop everything and come here."

"Dad! What's wrong with her?"

"Pneumonia. I told her she wasn't taking good enough care of herself. And she wasn't."

She sagged against Derrick in relief. "Are they taking care of her here? Is she getting better? What do they say?"

"They say her fever broke last night and she'll get better quickly now. She shouldn't have to stay more than a few days. Now, you tell me why you are here."

"You didn't cable what was wrong with her."

"Ah." His hand went to touch her consolingly. "I should have said, I guess, but they limit the words." He glanced curiously at Derrick.

"Dad, this is my—" She started to say boss, but he hadn't behaved much like one lately; he'd acted more like a friend. "This is Derrick Merchand. He brought me."

Parnell held out a hand. "Thank you, I appreciate it, but you needn't have. There was no emergency."

"No trouble," Derrick said. "Good to meet you."

"If everything is under control, why are you here, Dad? Why do you stay?"

"That's a silly question, Patty. Why not stay? I don't want to be anywhere else."

"But you need to get some rest. If you don't want

Mom to be alone, I'll stay and let you go home and get some sleep.''

''I've been nodding off all night. I don't need the rest as much as you look like you do.''

''You're right,'' Derrick said. ''She hasn't had any sleep for twenty-four hours.''

''Nor have you,'' Pat answered.

''I didn't faint yesterday.''

Parnell frowned at her. ''Why did you faint, Patty?''

She gave Derrick an accusing glance for bringing it up. ''Blood pressure dropped. I don't know. It isn't important. What I want is for you to go home and get some sleep.''

''Not a chance. If you want to stay a little while, I'll go shower and change, then come back. But then you're going to get some rest yourself. Right, Derrick?''

''Right. I'll run you home, Parnell. Patricia, I'll be back to get you.''

''But—''

''No buts. The issue is settled.'' He touched Parnell's arm, and they went toward the elevators.

Derrick was reminded strongly of when his mother had been ill. She had died a few years before his father, and Parnell was behaving much the way his father had: staying there, being near. He hadn't felt the loss of his mother as greatly as he had felt the loss of his father, because after his father died, he had no one. He still had no one.

As the two men got into the elevator Parnell glanced toward Patricia, standing in the doorway to his wife's room. ''She's a good girl,'' he said.

Derrick looked sharply at the older man. There was no denying that his interest in Pat had grown, but he still didn't trust her; he knew she wasn't a good girl. "I'll bet she gave you a lot of trouble with men and boys."

"No, not really. When she lived home, they were always hanging around, but she never gave us any trouble."

"But she's so—uh—pretty."

"That she is." He frowned. "Only time we were ever worried about her where men were concerned was when she first moved to New York. She got mixed up with a fellow there and thought she was going to marry him. Bad choice. Man was already married."

"VanStang," Derrick murmured.

"That's the one. She got out of the relationship, though, thank God. Learned her lesson too. He loaded her up with debts she hasn't paid off yet." He shook his head sadly and looked at Merchand. "I couldn't help her. I had too many debts of my own. Then Martha got sick, and Patty had to help us. Yes, she's a good girl."

Derrick tried to let the topic of Patricia's virtue settle as he followed Parnell's directions toward his home, but he couldn't. "She saw a lot of people when she was home for the holidays, though, didn't she?"

Parnell laughed at the question. "No. On New Year's we had to force her to go out with us; she went with a fellow she's known since high school." He chuckled again and glanced sideways at Derrick. "When midnight came, she wouldn't even let the poor guy kiss her."

"Wouldn't?" He found difficulty relating his perception of Patricia to her father's. He knew how wild and passionate she could be. She must have pulled the wool over her old man's eyes. He wanted to quiz Parnell, find out more about her, but he didn't want to be obvious and, mostly, he didn't want to admit his interest.

Parnell answered without being asked. "That was the only date Patty had all vacation. And she didn't let Lester drive her home that night; she said she had a headache and came home with us." He glanced at Derrick again. "Reckon there's someone in New York she's interested in? She doesn't say anything about anyone except those involved with her work. You're around her more than we are, perhaps you can tell me. Does she have many dates there? It seems like she works all the time, makes appearances with you. That right, son?"

"That's right," Derrick said uncomfortably. Maybe he was the one with the wool pulled over his eyes. But she had been so free and eager on the Key, and she hadn't known who he was—but she had stopped anything from happening too.

Dawn was beginning to make feeble inroads in the east when they reached the Dayton home. Parnell got out and stretched. "Want to go ahead and bring in your things?" he asked.

Derrick pulled out Pat's suitcase and started to follow Parnell to the door. "Get yours too, son. No need for you to try to drive back to New York until you get some sleep. You've been up as long as Patty."

"I thought I'd go to a hotel."

"Won't hear of it, we have a guest room; no need for you to go anywhere." Derrick didn't respond immediately, and Parnell said, "Let us offer you hospitality as a token of our gratefulness to you for looking after Patty. You flew our girl all the way back from Spain and, on top of that, you drove her all the way from New York so she could see her mother. Do stay, son."

He and Patricia had shared the same quarters for the past month or more and nothing had happened. Nothing would here either. And he was tired. It would be foolish not to stay. He got his case and followed Parnell into the house.

"You want a shower too?" Parnell asked. "There's a bath upstairs. Your room will be the one through the second door on the left. Patty's room is on the right. Bath is just beyond Patty's room."

"I think I will."

"Martha usually keeps the guest bed made up, but if it isn't, you can ask Patty for sheets when you bring her back."

"Right." Derrick started up the stairs.

"Towels are under the sink," Parnell called.

Derrick set his valise down in the hall and went into Patricia's room with hers. It was a definitely feminine room, and he had no doubt but that she'd chosen the color scheme: earth tones, pleasing to his eye. The room reflected the ages of her life. A worn stuffed panda bear was in a tiny chair in the corner, a high school pennant was on the wall, a pair of ice skates with their strings tied to make a loop were hung over a nail in the wall, and Merchand cosmetics were on her dressing table. He felt like an intruder snooping into her life, but he opened a few drawers anyway. She had moved away from home years ago, and the things inside weren't of a disclosing nature: old sweaters, worn slacks, junk jewelry. He shouldn't be nosy about her things. She was too real to him in here, and he didn't like those thoughts of permanence. He left the room in a hurry.

He put his case in the guest room, showered, shaved, and put on fresh clothes before he met Parnell downstairs. The older man looked refreshed by the short respite from his vigil.

"I'd like to get on back to the hospital if you don't mind," he said. "I'm sure you're hungry, but you can eat with Patty, and I can pick up something at the cafeteria there. What do you say?"

"Sounds like a winner."

When they reached Martha's room, Pat was dozing in the chair where Parnell had been. He smiled. "Told you she was tired," he said softly. He touched her shoulder. "Hey, daughter, wake up and go home to bed. I'm back."

Pat looked at him hazily. "Hi, Dad. Okay."

"Did she wake?" He nodded toward his wife.

"Uh-uh. Slept right on. Nurse came in once to check her out, but even that didn't bother her."

"She had a sleeping pill." He smiled. "I don't think you're going to need one. Go get some rest, then you can come back this evening and relieve me for a while. Martha's out of danger, but I think I'll spend nights with her."

"You should have a cot brought in."

"I will. Now, you and Derrick run along. And feed him, Pat. He hasn't eaten." He leaned to kiss her cheek. "See you this evening."

As Derrick helped Patricia into the car he said, "Your father offered to let me stay in the guest room."

"Fine." She yawned. "He must like you."

She drifted to sleep on the drive home, and Derrick was glad he had paid attention when he'd gone with Parnell; he'd have hated to wake her to ask directions. He did wake her when they got to the house—he woke her trying not to. He was lifting her out of her seat to carry her to bed.

"I can walk," she murmured. But she leaned heavily on him. They were at her bedroom door when she said. "Oh! Breakfast. Dad said to feed you."

"I don't want to eat now, Patricia. I'm so tired, I could drop. Let's sleep first, then eat. Okay?"

She smiled. "Good idea. The state I'm in, I'd probably burn everything."

He impulsively bent and kissed her. "'Night, Pat." In haste he backed away: he wasn't *that* tired or sleepy.

Her eyes suddenly lost their drowsiness. "G'night. See you later." She went into her room quickly and shut the door.

Patricia slept almost all day, and when she woke she was nauseated. She almost didn't make it to the bathroom in time. She felt dreadful. She had been working too hard and steadily, had been worrying too much and not sleeping enough. After she could stand, she put a damp rag on her head and within minutes felt better, but dark circles stained the skin beneath her eyes. It was a good thing they'd put off taking pictures for a while; she'd need the magic of Merchand cosmetics to cover this dilapidated state.

When she came out of the bath, Derrick was in the hall. "Are you all right?" he asked. "I heard you in there."

She wanted to crunch into a small wad in the corner. "I'm sorry. I'm fine now. I guess I'm more tired than I thought, and my emotions affect me that way sometimes." She tried to smile. "I'm okay."

"You haven't eaten. I should have made you breakfast before you went to sleep. I probably wouldn't have burned it any more than you would have."

"You can cook?"

"Sure I can. Show me where the kitchen is and I'll prove it."

"I don't believe you. You probably have a cook to tend to you the way your driver did." Pat waved her hand. "Let there be food."

"I didn't always have one. I went to university, you know. Had the same hardships as everyone."

"I'll bet. Only two servants."

"Oh, more than that. But I gave them weekends off and had to fend for myself then or starve to death." He took her arm. "Come show me the kitchen."

"Let me put something on."

"I thought you had something on." He looked at her fuzzy dacron robe.

"Something else."

"Okay."

He watched her go into her room and shut the door, but he talked to her through it. "Actually, I didn't have servants when I was in college. I had an apartment and it had a little kitchen and I did a lot of cooking. Especially breakfasts. Simplest meal of the day." He couldn't recall ever having been so open with a woman before, so loquacious—with anyone, actually, man or woman. But she was distressed because he'd heard her being sick, and he wanted her to be at ease, to know he still liked her. "Then in New York when my father was alive, I had my own place and only a cleaning woman. I had to cook then. It was only after I went back to the family mansion that I got spoiled."

He hadn't got spoiled, he simply hadn't had time for anything but the corporation and work. He should be at work now, but it was so easy not to go. Things had run smoothly for as long as he'd been in Europe, and they'd expected him to be gone for another couple of weeks.

"And besides," he said through the door, "I'm so hungry, I could eat anyone's cooking. Including mine."

Pat came out dressed in slacks and a shirt in the earth tones he liked so much on her. "Me too," she said. "Let's go."

In the brightly lit yellow-and-white kitchen Patricia got the utensils as Derrick took eggs and bacon, butter and jelly, from the refrigerator.

"How many pieces for you?" she asked as she put the bacon on to fry.

"Four, and three eggs. I'm a starving man. And I like my eggs over easy. I can't stand hard yolk."

"Me either."

She put a fresh tablecloth on the corner table and laid it with flatware and condiments.

"Candles," Derrick said. "We must have candles."

"They are on the dining room table."

"We want to be as festive as possible. This is the first time we've breakfasted together, but I must say I—"

But he didn't say. He left the sentence hanging, and she had to surmise he'd been going to say he hadn't expected to share breakfast with her under such innocent circumstances.

When the bacon was crisp, Pat put it on paper to drain and began the eggs. "Darn," she said as the yolk broke. She tried again and broke the second yolk as well. "Damn," she said this time.

He chuckled. "You said all I had to worry about was burned food. Well, no one ever said they liked the yolks of scrambled eggs runny." He took a fork and stirred the eggs. "Quick! Salt, pepper, more eggs."

She rushed to get what he ordered.

"Plates," he commanded and, after he ladled the eggs onto them, said, "See? Perfect scrambled eggs. I told you I could cook."

"So you did." She got the toaster and put it on the table where it would be within easy reach.

Derrick began without waiting for her. "I must admit you do all right with bacon, even though you're a failure with eggs."

When they were finished, he said, "That'll do for an appetizer."

"Appetizer! I couldn't eat another bite."

"You'll be able to after we visit your mother and give Parnell a break. I'll take you out so we won't have to fight over who gets to cook."

She smiled at him. "I guess I'll be able to eat again then. Here, help me with this mess."

"Me?" he asked incredulously.

"Yes, you. You helped make it. Put the things back in the fridge, and I'll put the dishes in the dishwasher."

"Now I remember why I have servants," he said. "This part isn't much fun."

But he seemed to enjoy helping clean up as much as he had helping mess up.

Martha was awake and the tube was gone from her nose, but the IV was still in place. She was sitting, propped by the tilted bed. She paid little attention to her daughter. "Parnell told me you brought our Patty all the way here from Spain. I want to thank you for that," she said to Derrick, then smiled. "I thought I was going to die, but Parnell wouldn't let me. He hauled me in here again."

"You should be glad he did. Pneumonia isn't something to ignore; it's a serious illness."

"If I didn't believe it before, I do now. I'm weak as a baby."

"You're my baby," Parnell said. "My baby doll."

Martha smiled at him, then turned her attention back to Derrick. "My daughter tells me you're quite the businessman; you've done a lot for your company, and your cosmetics are making great inroads."

"Your daughter is a very astute young lady if she said that, because it's true." He glanced at Patricia. "She was no minor help in getting the cosmetic line on its feet."

"You aren't married, are you, Derrick?"

Pat could scarcely keep from groaning at her mother's flagrance—and she was struck with a stab of remembered anger and pain because of what Derrick had said the night she had gone to bed with him.

"No, I'm not," he said. "Parnell, why don't I take you somewhere for dinner." He gave Patricia a look that told her more than words could that he had no honorable intentions toward her whatsoever, and what's more, he didn't even have dishonorable ones anymore.

She bristled, but in front of her sick mother she couldn't very well yell at him or throw things. And besides, all she wanted to do was weep. Damn. Bart Van-Stang had been a better choice than Derrick Merchand would ever be. At least Bart had pretended to care a little—and he would have cared as long as she would have financed him.

As soon as the men left she turned to her mother. "How *could* you, Mom? Ask him if he was married? How obvious."

"I was curious."

"When I was home for Christmas, I told you he wasn't."

Her mother looked ultimately innocent. "I forgot."

"He's a confirmed bachelor and he wants no ties with anyone. I know that most clearly."

"He likes you. He brought you home."

"He puts up with me, that's all. The only reason he brought me was because he felt guilty at making me work so hard. There's nothing else, believe me."

"Then why didn't he put you on a train in New York?"

"I was worried, nearly frantic, I thought— Well, never mind what I thought. But there weren't any good connections. It was simply a case of an employer being considerate of an employee; no more."

"How do you feel about him?"

Pat went to the bed crank and began to turn it. "Want me to lower you awhile, Mom? Are you tired sitting up?"

"How do you feel about him, Patty? Are you in love with him?"

"Gracious, Mother." She continued to churn the crank. "Why? Do I act like I'm in love with him? Have I said anything to make you think it?"

"No. Not really. I just wondered."

"He's a very attractive man and he's my boss; that's all there is and that's all there's going to be."

The bed was now down as far as it would go. "Patty, I don't want to be flat, I want to sit up."

"Oh. Sorry." She began to turn the crank the other way.

"Do you like him?"

"Who?"

"Mr. Merchand," she said. "Derrick," she added, knowing her daughter was being purposefully obtuse. "Do you like him?"

"Sometimes. Sometimes not. He's okay, I guess. Can we change the subject?"

"Sure," Martha said, smiling. "Did you enjoy Europe? Did you have time to sightsee? Did you get to see the Eiffel Tower? I've always wanted to see it. Was it as wonderful as I think it ought to be?"

"Probably more so. I know it was to me." Pat couldn't separate thoughts of Europe from thoughts of Merchand: they were too tightly interwoven. But she couldn't ask to change the subject again. Actually, there wasn't anything she could talk about that didn't remind her of him.

Three and a half hours passed before Parnell and Derrick returned. They were warm and relaxed with each other.

Derrick took Patricia to eat, and later they watched the late news. They went upstairs together, and at her door he told her good night and kissed her fondly, as a brother would. He was thinking she was tied by that clause in the contract and couldn't marry for two more years. He might decide then wasn't too soon; he'd be thirty-seven, almost thirty-eight. Not too bad. Not too soon. He could forgive her for having known Van-Stang. Parnell had eased his mind on that score, *and* the association had occurred before she'd come to work for him. He still had difficulty accepting the way she had behaved on Otter Key. Of course, he'd been the man on the island, but she hadn't known that. He would think about it. He had two years. He didn't have to make a sudden decision.

In the morning she was ill again. When Derrick heard her in the bathroom, he was concerned but didn't linger in the hallway; she'd been upset because he was there the day before.

He made coffee and had his suitcase beside the front door before she came downstairs. "Coffee?"

"Yes, thanks."

As he poured her a cup he said, "You were sick again this morning, weren't you?"

"I think I must have picked up a bug somewhere. Or it could be all the foreign food I've been eating. I'm not accustomed to it."

"Could be," he said. "You ought get Martha's doctor to look at you."

"I've had a stomach virus before. It'll go away."

"Have him look at you. We don't want Merchand's girl out of commission very long." Pat glanced at him, and he realized what he'd said. Well, she was—in a way.

"All right," she said. "If I'm not better soon, I'll have him give me the once-over. But my nausea is probably caused by worry and fatigue and a screwed-up sleep schedule."

"Maybe. But you fainted too. Ask him. Promise me."

"All right. If I have a recurrence of any kind, I will."

"Good." Derrick headed for the door. "You have to cook your own breakfast this morning. Sorry about that." He smiled. "If I stay, you'll make me clean up." He got so blasted homey when he was in this house with her, and when he was with Parnell or visiting her mother. He had to get out of here before he began to think thirty-five wasn't too soon to marry. "Parnell said your mother should be home in a couple of days. so I'm going to anticipate you'll be back in New York next week and make the England plans accordingly." He shut the door behind him and he was outside and safe.

Chapter Seventeen

Within a few days Martha was able to go home and, though weak, she was recuperating nicely. Pat hadn't had a recurrence of her nausea and was confident her seizures had been caused by something she'd eaten—or were in reaction to worry and fatigue—or were a physical manifestation of her distress at being so utterly drawn to Derrick and so hopelessly unable to do anything about it.

She returned to the city. Her apartment seemed unfamiliar to her: new, larger than she recalled, and empty.

Pat phoned Russell to say she was back, and he said Merchand would be in touch with her. He didn't say where Derrick was or how he was or when he'd be in touch, but she had no intention of going out, because she might miss the chance to exchange a few words with him. She dusted, straightened the apartment, changed the linens. She called Becky, who was vibrating with the news that she'd landed a supporting role in an Off-Broadway production.

"Morris is dying with envy," Becky said, "but he's proud of me too." She asked about the tour and about Derrick and about Pat's folks. She invited her over, but Pat wouldn't leave the nearness of the phone.

It was nine o'clock before Derrick called. He wanted to know if she was all right, and if she'd be ready to leave for London in a couple of days. He said he was catching up on a backlog of work and that he'd be going to England too.

Pat didn't see him before she caught the plane, but when she was settled in her window seat, she waited eagerly for him to appear. A stranger took the place beside her. She was surprised—and disappointed—and was reminded again that she only worked for the man.

Nonstop from New York to London, she fretted. What if he were different? What if she were different? What if they'd met sooner, later, never at all? What if he loved her? Her what if's were as pointless and as unending as her fantasies had been.

Derrick was waiting when she landed, and he smiled when he saw her. She could scarcely keep from running to him, but when she reached him, he was as much her boss as ever. He said he had come a day early to set up the schedule so it would be easier on her and that he'd rented a car so they could drive in England and Scotland. He asked how her mother was, how her father was, how she was.

And again they had separate rooms in the same suite.

It seemed to her she had her picture taken all over London, then they left the city and drove west through Oxford, then turned north to go through Stow on the Wold and Moreton in the Marsh. They could have got to Coventry more directly by driving north from London, and she asked him about the route.

"I wanted you to see those places," he said. "You wouldn't have believed the names existed otherwise."
He was the friend he'd been in Europe, he made no

sexual innuendos, didn't try to kiss her. And Pat was distraught.

She did commercials in The Midlands, on the moors, in the Cotswold Hills, and in the Lake District. When they went to Edinburgh, their suite had a view of the castle: romantic and beautiful. The sight didn't change Derrick's attitude toward her one bit. She had her picture taken there and at Loch Ness and on the Firth of Clyde.

The unaccustomed food or the work schedule or the residual worry about her mother or the strain and tension of being too near Merchand caused her nausea to return. But she had worked hard before and eaten strange food before and been worried before; but never had she been so near someone she was so drawn to. She was sure Derrick was the reason for her illness. Their sharing of a suite had to stop. She preferred fantasy to the inaccessibility of him.

On the last night in Scotland they went to dinner together: and alone. Every other night, one or more of the local artists or businessmen had been with them. As they waited for their food Derrick explained that on the next day they were to leave for Ireland and he had no further need to discuss business.

He made that excuse because he didn't want her to know he wanted to be alone with her. Before, he'd invented reasons for people to be with them, but the truth was, he didn't trust himself. Patricia had become too prevalent on his mind. He remembered how right he had felt when he made love to her—and he was terrified it would happen again.

"I understand," Pat said. Less than a week, she was thinking; only a few more days to endure the torment of having him so near.

In strained silence they finished dinner. When they returned to the suite, instead of leaving her near the center of the room, Derrick strolled with her toward her door. As she started to open it he touched her shoulder gently. "I—" He stopped. Then his head dipped toward her. "Patricia." His lips touched hers lightly. "Good night." He took a step away, but his arm reached behind to catch her; he turned and his arms went around her and his mouth met hers.

Pat melded against him, touching him with every part of her body that could touch him. She clutched him desperately, and he was clutching too.

"Patricia." His lips searched her face and came to her ear. "I want you," he whispered.

"It was a mistake. You said it was a mistake."

"It wasn't; it was right. Much too right. The only mistake made was when I said that. I need you, Patricia. Please."

Derrick moved her to the couch and began to unbutton her blouse. When it was undone, he pulled it from her waistband and lowered her. "You're beautiful, do you know that?" He took off his jacket and shirt as she slipped her blouse off and pitched it to the floor. When he was bare from the waist up, she pushed him backward, fastened her mouth to his, and snuggled on top of him, where she belonged again.

"You're so comfortable," he murmured.

She had never felt so comfortable or so relieved, and she relished the smell and taste and touch of him. She didn't think about tomorrow, now had all her concentration. They were touching each other with flesh, with stocking-covered feet; kissing, nibbling, licking each other.

They got up suddenly—both of them—and shed the

rest of their clothes, then they were back on the couch with him on top. Their touching became less investigatory, more possessive, until each was frantic.

"Come here," she said, so weakly he might not have heard. "Come here!" Louder. She was dying for him

She felt every molecule of her awakening and she was in rapture, in ecstasy.

Euphoria had taken over again and she was aware only of surges of delight. She'd had him only once before and she didn't know if she'd ever have him again She was insatiable. The hard thrust of the ending of his climb drove her to frenzy, but he didn't stop; he kept on until she was warm and wanted and complete.

Derrick was with her, her arms were around him; she could smell the scent of him, feel his chest move as he breathed, and if she opened her eyes, she'd be able to see him. She did and was seized by tumbling nausea. She couldn't repress it. She shoved him aside and darted to her room and through it to the bathroom.

He was only a second behind her, and his hand cupped her brow. When she eased, he left her a moment, dampened a cloth, and held it for her.

"I'm all right," she said, panting.

"Did you ever go to the doctor?"

"I was fine until I started eating the food over here." This wasn't pleasant—talking to him with her head hung over the bowl of a toilet.

"Did you see a doctor?"

"No."

"You're going to one today."

Pat smiled weakly. "It isn't day. It's night."

"Then you'll see one tonight."

"I'll be all right." She took the cloth and wiped her mouth. "I'm sorry."

"You're going to a doctor, Patricia, and I won't listen to any refusals. Wash and get dressed."

"I feel better now. Really, I do. It must have been the haggis we tried." She knew her emotions had got to her. She was tied in knots all the time because of her feelings for Derrick, and after they had made love and were lying together, she had known she couldn't bear the thought of losing him.

"I said I wouldn't listen to refusals." His eyes sparked with command. "Get showered. I'll get a line on a doctor."

She started to say she wanted to wait until they were back in the States, but he glared at her. "Dammit! Do as I say!"

Derrick left the small room and, as he went, she realized this was the first time she'd seen him walk without his clothes. Or was it? The way he moved seemed so familiar. But in her apartment, she'd gone from him.

Before she turned on the shower she heard him on the phone. By the time she was ready, he was dressed and waiting in the sitting room.

"You look better," he said.

"I told you it was something I ate."

"The doctor will be here soon."

"I really don't need one. I feel fine now."

He started toward her, then stopped. "God," he said softly. "And you fainted."

"I know. I remember. You must think I'm terribly unhealthy, but I'm not. I was tired then."

"You were sick in the mornings."

"I was fatigued. And I was worried."

He sat abruptly in the nearest chair. "When was your last period?"

Pat turned pale. What was he thinking? "I don't know."

"When was it?"

"I don't recall." She couldn't. She'd been busy with the tour and her mother's illness and thinking about Derrick. She hadn't paid attention. She *could* have missed. "Really, I don't remember."

"Your symptoms are common to pregnancy: normal."

"I can't be pregnant."

Derrick's shoulders relaxed. "You can't?"

"Well, not—not *can't*. I shouldn't be."

"Shouldn't?" He was tense again. "You didn't take care?"

She shook her head. "But I can't be pregnant." He was the only one who could be the father. A new wave of nausea almost overtook her—for a totally different reason this time. He would kill her. "I can't," she whispered.

He was quiet a minute. "Whose is it?"

She glanced at him.

"Oh, no, you don't. We've only— Twice. And the second time was just now."

"It only takes once," she said dryly.

Derrick looked at her, totally disbelieving. "That doesn't happen anymore. Not even in dime novels."

He was defending himself before she'd thought of accusing him, before they knew if she was pregnant. Furious, she said, "There are no dime novels anymore. Have you priced one lately?"

"You can't trap me," he said. "Oh, no. I was falling in love with you, but I won't be trapped."

"Sure," she shouted. "I took my temperature every

day so I'd know exactly when to get you in the sack. I planned it. I tricked you into it. That's all I ever wanted: to make someone have to marry me." She pulled herself erect. "But if I had done that, it wouldn't have been to you. I'd have done it to someone I wanted to marry."

"Women are supposed to take care of that sort of thing. You didn't get pregnant when you were with Bart."

"Right. Because I didn't take any chances. Women only take care of 'that sort of thing' if there are going to be any reasons to take care of it. I didn't know there would be."

"You didn't, didn't you?"

"No, I didn't." Tears came suddenly to her eyes. She knew he'd never believe he was the father, and she knew he had to be. Derrick didn't trust her—never had. And she didn't want that kind of relationship with anyone. "Look at the bright side," she said. "You can fire me now. I know you've been wanting a reason."

"No. It's you who wanted a reason. That's why you got pregnant. Well, they don't have to take full-body shots, they can get just your face. Your look. And you'll have that look, pregnant or not."

"I'll gain weight," she said coldly. "That's grounds for you to fire me. I don't think I could possibly keep from gaining weight."

"Yes, it's grounds, but I don't *have* to fire you. You'll stay the Merchand Girl." He slumped helplessly in his chair. "Dammit, why did you have to get pregnant?"

"We don't even know if I did get pregnant," she screamed, "but if I did, for sure it was all a deliberate plan, all premeditated to get me out of my contract."

"You can't *do* that, though, now, can you?" he said with a quick glare at her.

"I don't know why you want me to stay on. You ought to be glad you have an excuse to let me go."

"Dammit, Patricia, I—" He stopped abruptly. He'd started to say: I love you and I can't bear to think of you not connected with me and my work. He put his face in his hands to keep himself from speaking. He did love her, and if she was pregnant, only he could be the father. He'd been with her daily and nearly every evening for three months except for the time when she had gone home for the Christmas holidays, and Parnell had said she'd stayed close to them all that time; she had gone out only once and then returned home with her parents. She couldn't have conceived with anyone else. And he hadn't been going to think of marrying her for two more years. Now he had to think of it.

"Yes. Dammit," she said. "Damn you! I don't even know if I am pregnant. You're the one who decided I was expecting, and you're the one who, in your conceit and egotism, bravely jumped to the conclusion that if I was pregnant, the baby had to be yours. I never said it."

He uncovered his face and looked at her. "Whose would it be, then?"

"I don't think that should concern you, since you're convinced it couldn't be yours."

He leaped from his chair and grabbed her and shook her. "Whose is it, then? If not mine, whose?"

Pat wanted to hit him, and cry, and die; she was vastly miserable. He was killing her. "If you must know, the father is the man from Otter Key."

Derrick shoved her from him so quickly, she nearly lost her balance. "He is not."

"He is. Maybe he lied and said nothing happened, but something did."

"What's his name, then? Huh? Tell me that."

She couldn't answer and she wouldn't look at him. "It's none of your business."

"I think it is."

"Why? So you can go make him marry me? No, thank you!"

For a moment he watched her without speaking. Then he said, "I'll marry you."

"You'll what?" Pat was so incensed, her voice cracked. "You'll do no such thing. I'm not trying to get you to marry me. I don't want you to marry me. I don't want to marry you."

"Nonetheless, you'll do it."

"I'll do no such thing. What makes you think I will? And the contract forbids it."

"I know what the damn contract says. I wrote it."

"I'm fully aware of that fact."

"I can write another."

"I won't sign it."

"You'll do anything I want you to do."

"You are out of your mind! We don't even know if I'm pregnant, and you don't think it's yours if I am. But if I am carrying a bundle of joy, I admit it isn't yours. It was the man on Otter Key. You're off the hook."

Derrick cocked an eyebrow at her, went back to his seat, lounged into the chair, and crossed his legs in front of him. "I was the man on Otter Key."

"You?" She laughed, half-hysterically. "You were not."

"Oh?"

Memories flooded back to her: She'd thought Merchand's walk was familiar; the fisherman's voice had sounded like his; he'd known how to touch her; he wanted light when they made love in her apartment, saying he wanted to see her this time. *This time.* "You're crazy," she said, still denying what she was beginning to believe.

"Why in the world do you think I had those two clauses put in the contract? I wanted to tie you up, keep you available, know where you were all the time. I knew how you could behave. Twice you did it."

"How do you know that?"

"I told you. I was the man on the beach."

"He couldn't have been you."

"He was."

"Then why didn't you say anything? Why didn't you say *something*?"

"I did. The first time I offered to exchange names, but you said we should stay with no names."

He had been there. "Then why were you so angry with me? When I came back from Disney World, you acted as though you thought I was no more than a tramp, and not to be trusted out of your sight."

"Well, are you?" He sat straight. "*Are* you? You didn't know he was me, and you were going to make love. I was so damn jealous, I could have killed you."

"But I didn't do anything with—with—"

"Me! With me! But that was only because I was so mad at you, I wouldn't."

"It was because I didn't know he was you that I wouldn't."

"But you went into his arms," Derrick said, plaintive, hurt, and bereft.

"Oh, Derrick, I did that because I was trying to forget you."

"You hadn't met me the first time you did it," he said, still wretched. "Why did you behave so wild and sensuous then?"

"For the same reason," she said softly. "I'd got into the habit of dreaming, of fantasizing. I used to get the proper expression for the camera by living in a dream-world, and I thought a dose of reality would make me stop."

Now he had a dream to envy. But she'd said used to; that was the way she *used* to get the proper expression. "How do you get your look now?" he asked, but he knew; he'd known since the day she made that Christmas commercial: she thought of him. "I know how," he said softly as he rose and went to her. "By thinking of me."

"I've always thought of you."

"Even before you met me?"

"Yes. Even then. He just didn't have a name."

He put his arms around her "I want to go back to the island with you, I want to make love with you there Say you will. We can stay at my house."

She frowned. "Do you own that house?"

"Yes."

"Then you lied. You said you didn't live there."

"I don't. I live in New York."

"You're qualifying."

"I'm asking you to marry me, Pat. Now. Soon. And we can honeymoon on Otter Key."

"You don't have to marry me; I don't think I'm pregnant. I make myself sick when I'm under emotional stress."

"I'll marry you anyway—and get you pregnant."

"But you don't want to marry. You're not the marrying kind. Remember?"

"I've changed my mind. I love you, Patricia. I've never loved anyone the way I love you. I didn't know what love was until I met you."

The only person who had ever said those things to her was her fantasy lover. She looked at Derrick, at his hazel eyes, at his lips waiting to be kissed, and she knew every dream she'd ever had was coming true. "I'll marry you," she said, leaning toward him, starting to kiss him, feeling content; then she stopped. "But that contract between us will be for life."

Derrick smiled. "If it weren't, I'd add a clause or two."

"You would, wouldn't you?" She let her lips touch his, and his mouth was real, so real, she knew she'd never need another fantasy.

Enter a uniquely exciting new world with

Harlequin American Romance™

Harlequin American Romances are the first romances to explore today's love relationships. These compelling novels reach into the hearts and minds of women across America... probing the most intimate moments of romance, love and desire.

You'll follow romantic heroines and irresistible men as they boldly face confusing choices. Career first, love later? Love without marriage? Long-distance relationships? All the experiences that make love real are captured in the tender, loving pages of **Harlequin American Romances.**

What makes American women so different when it comes to love? Find out with **Harlequin American Romance!**

Send for your introductory FREE book now!

Get this book FREE!

Mail to:

Harlequin Reader Service

In the U.S.	In Canada
2504 West Southern Avenue	649 Ontario Street
Tempe, AZ 85282	Stratford, Ontario N5A 6W2

YES! I want to be one of the first to discover **Harlequin American Romance.** Send me FREE and without obligation *Twice in a Lifetime.* If you do not hear from me after I have examined my·FREE book, please send me the 4 new **Harlequin American Romances** each month as soon as they come off the presses. I understand that I will be billed only $2.25 for each book (total $9.00). There are no shipping or handling charges. There is no minimum number of books that I have to purchase. In fact, I may cancel this arrangement at any time. *Twice in a Lifetime* is mine to keep as a FREE gift, even if I do not buy any additional books.

Name   (please print)

Address   Apt. no.

City   State/Prov.   Zip/Postal Code

Signature (If under 18, parent or guardian must sign.)